WARNING

This book contains sexually explicit scenes and adult language. It may be considered offensive to some readers. This book is for sale to adults ONLY.

* * * * * * * * * * * * * * * * * *

Please store your files wisely where they cannot be accessed by underage readers.

DISCLAIMER

ISBN-13: 978-1988083155
ISBN-10: 198808315X

Other Books by Darla Dunbar:

<u>The Romeo Alpha BBW Paranormal Shifter Romance Series</u>

Amanda Walker thinks that she has a normal and boring life. That is until after her 24th birthday. Everything changes when she meets the man who says he was supposed to be her husband. Denying everything the man says, she fights him every step of the way. But after he kidnaps her, Amanda discovers that there are some things about her family that her parents kept a secret all these years. Among the history of the family she learns secrets she thought only happened in story books. Can Amanda tell the difference between truth and lies or is she this mysterious woman that holds the key to a legacy?

<u>Romeo Alpha Blood Lines Romance Series</u>

Twenty-four years have passed in relative peace for Amanda and Romeo. They've raised five children into adulthood and are thoroughly enjoying their lives as the Alpha King and Queen of the werewolves. At twenty-four, Sarina is just stepping into her powers and will be ripe for mating when her birthday comes in two weeks. What no one knows is the danger that lurks just outside their tight knit community. Romeo has made peace with the other clans and has enjoyed that peace, but it will all come crashing down around him when his oldest daughter comes of age to take a mate.

The Alpha Feud BBW Paranormal Shifter Romance Series

Eliza's life consisted of reporting on boring, crowd-pleasing events, like their country livestock fair. With the arrival of two handsome brothers, the lives of Eliza and her best friend, Melissa, are shaken to the core. For Eliza, the arrival of this new man becomes a test of her relationship with her current boyfriend, who she's been happily living with for over six years. Does Hayden, a complete stranger, really wield the power to make Eliza reconsider her relationship with Andrew?

The Daemon Paranormal Romance Chronicles

The daemon infighting can only be stopped when a strong leader emerges to calm the different factions. Juno appears to be at the heart of the conflict. Things become complicated when Phoebe and Supay try to negotiate with the siren, Juno. The love triangle among Phoebe, Supay and Apollo become tense when Juno's meddling threatens to destroy any romance that develops.

The Mind Talker Paranormal Romance Series

Ananda finds herself on the run and she's not alone. With help from Jared, a stranger that she just met, the two evade capture by an organization that is intent on hunting her kind. Ananda and Jared are able to read minds. When an unfortunate incident happened involving a disturbed individual that resulted in the death of his schoolmates, the secret organization decided to take action.

<u>The Leather Satchel Paranormal Romance Series</u>

Valtina is stuck in Middle World, unable to pass on to The Afterlife. In order to redeem herself from past deeds done, she must help bring romance back into the world and stop The Dark Side from destroying love in its entirety. Following orders issued by Ladaya and armed with a leather satchel filled with the appropriate tools and weapons, Valtina embraces each mission with enthusiasm.

Get the latest update on new releases from the author at:

https://darladunbar.com/newsletter/

This book is Part One of the "The Alpha Packed BBW Paranormal Shifter Romance Series"

Book 1

Darlene has led a quiet life since suffering through a terrible break-up. She wants nothing more than to spend her time in front of the TV, away from any sort of trouble. But all that goes down the drain when handsome, rugged and rough Idris comes into her life. He is a werewolf on the lookout for his missing pack leader. Darlene quickly finds herself pulled towards this mysterious man and at the same time finds herself falling deeper and deeper into the world of the supernatural.

Book 2

Darlene finally has Idris all to herself. But with forces outside her control threatening her safety, will she be able to juggle both Idris and her newfound powers? Idris is being threatened with exile over telling Darlene about his world. With pressure mounting from both packs, he tries to protect Darlene from whatever he can. But Vivica, his old vampire girlfriend, will stop at nothing to get him back into her life – or else.

Book 3

With Idris facing a life time as an Exsul, Darlene finds herself trying to cope with her own power of seeing and connecting with spirits. Idris is tormented by his life choices and where he ends up at the risk of shoving Darlene away from him. Then Idris' maker turns up on his doorstep with a seductive promise – to lead a pack of Exsuls for the purpose of changing the future of all werewolves to come. Will Idris and Darlene be able to survive these trying times?

Book 4

Just as Darlene thinks her life has settled down, a terrible old foe returns for revenge. Darlene is still learning how to control her abilities with the spirit world when Jacob returns with an army of his own werewolf/vampire hybrid creatures. He has only one goal... get his revenge on Darlene and the packs that ruined his plan with Lucian the first time around. Darlene and Idris find themselves fighting for survival for the final time – but will they both survive?

A BBW Paranormal Shifter Romance Series

Alpha Packed

Book One

By Darla Dunbar

Table of Contents

Chapter One 1
Chapter Two 11
Chapter Three 22
Chapter Four 35
Chapter Five 53
Chapter Six 62
Chapter Seven 74
Chapter Eight 89
Chapter Nine 105
Chapter Ten 117
Chapter Eleven 126
Chapter Twelve 143
Chapter Thirteen 160
Other Books by Darla Dunbar 191
About the Author - Darla Dunbar 192
Connect with Darla Dunbar 193

Chapter One

THIS WAS a huge mistake. Darlene should have known better, but in utter and total desperation, she agreed to this date. Now the guy in front of her—what was his name again? Steve? Mike? She couldn't even remember now—had been talking non-stop about pro wrestling. But not even actual real wrestling. The stuff that was fake and basically just soap operas with some terrible phony fights thrown in.

"So then the Ice Cube challenged The Man to a battle!"

"Wow, really?" Darlene replied, feigning interest on every possible level.

This was her mistake. She had been spending way too much time at home lately, curled up on the couch, binge watching reality television shows because they made her feel better about her boring life. Darlene would leave for work in the mornings, do eight hours at a boring local bookstore, come home, eat and watch TV. She also stayed up far later than any normal human should, which resulted in limited forms of social communication.

That was how Darlene ended up on some free dating website. She deleted most of the messages she got. They were mostly from guys who seemed to think of her as a sexual fetish instead of an actual human being. Getting messages from guys who were into her being overweight made her feel uncomfortable. Darlene either got disgusted looks or sexual lust over her size. Both sucked. She had been about to delete her page for good when a guy who appeared to be normal messaged her. He hadn't made any gross comments about her size and even made her laugh once or twice with his messages. It had been eight months since her last relationship blew up in her face. *Why not try something different?* She decided to accept his date.

The guy was so boring that Darlene wished the restaurant would go up in flames so she could flee. She was flipping through her options on how to end the date early when he finally pushed his plate away.

"That was delicious," he said.

"Oh yeah. It was great," Darlene lied, thinking the potatoes were too dry for her liking.

The check came and the guy—what was his name!—made an effort to search for his wallet. *Oh here we go...*

"Oh man. I forgot my wallet at home!" he said with fake surprise.

"Yeah, yeah, I got it," she mumbled, slamming her debit card on the table.

It didn't take a genius to figure out this asshole had asked her out to throw her what he thought was a "pity date" and get a free meal out of her. He would probably go home to all his idiot friends and talk about how he gave the fat girl a date because he was just so nice. Darlene felt like punching him in the face.

She paid, and they walked out of the restaurant in silence. He escorted her to her car and then glanced around, as if checking so that no one could see him, before he tried to kiss her.

"Yeah," Darlene lifted up her hand to block him, "I don't think so. Thanks for nothing though, seriously."

The man scowled and before he could say something back, Darlene got into her car. She pulled out of the parking lot as quickly as she could, wanting to forget the entire terrible date.

What a mistake. What an absolute mistake. Not even just the date. The last couple years of her life had been a huge mistake. She wished she could travel back in time and re-do everything. The first thing she'd do would be to say a resounding *no* when Austin proposed to her.

Darlene pulled into her apartment complex five minutes later. She had picked a nearby restaurant so she could make a quick escape home if needed. She walked up to the second floor. The couple by the stairwell was fighting again. They were constantly screaming at each other over everything. Some nights, Darlene wanted to yell back at them to just break up. Other times, she wanted to tell them to make it work, because being alone was terrible.

She opened the front door of her apartment and glanced around. Her computer was on in one corner, and a few blankets were thrown on the couch for maximum comfort for those times when she drowned herself in ice cream and terrible reality shows. Everything else was clean though. Darlene couldn't stand her apartment being messy or dirty. She wanted it to be perfect, as if she could make her apartment look like how she didn't feel.

Darlene yanked off her high heels and plopped down in front of her computer. She deleted the online dating profile and stared out the window. That was it — she was going to become a hermit. Well, as much of a hermit as one can be if they still had to go to work and grocery shop and run errands…but other than that she was totally going to be a hermit from now on. People were not her thing. People were just terrible all around. And she'd had enough of terrible people.

She moved to the couch, wrapping herself up in a blanket. Darlene mused over what she would watch. Terrible shows about being tricked into online dating seemed like a good end to the night. It'd make her feel better at the very least.

Her cellphone rang loudly. Darlene jolted awake, startled. She wasn't used to her new ringtone. It used to be the theme song of an old cartoon she liked, but after everything went to hell she changed it to a normal ring in an effort to seem more adult. Now the ring was bleating loudly and annoying her. She looked at the front of the screen… her boss.

"Hello?"

"Hey, sorry, did I wake you?"

"No, Maria," Darlene lied. "What's up?"

"I had to fire Jacob. Can you cover his shift? You'd be working till three."

Darlene glanced at the clock to see it was a little past eight in the morning. "That's fine. I'll leave now."

She hopped in the shower, letting the warm water rush over her. She wasn't surprised that Maria had to fire Jacob. He was constantly late and unable to help any of the customers who came into the shop. The bookstore was small and dealt with books that couldn't be found at any of the chains. Business was slow, but the books were rare enough that Maria only needed to sell a few each month to keep the business going. Darlene liked how quiet it was and the fact that human interaction was minimal. She knew she needed to get over this slump she was in, but felt no desire to. Almost everything Darlene did as of late seemed to feed into it — her lifestyle, her job, even the stupid things she spent time watching and looking up online.

The bookstore was only a ten-minute drive to downtown and located between a coffee shop and a cheesy massage parlor. Maria hated the massage parlor. She thought it was tacky and ruined the charm of the street. Darlene usually liked to watch to see how many guys went in there. She swore it was a front for some hookers.

Darlene parked her car and headed toward the bookshop. She could already tell no one was in the store. She walked inside and waved to Maria.

"Oh, I am so glad you are here!" Maria exclaimed when she saw Darlene. "I'll have to hire someone right away, but you and I will have to work extra in the meantime."

"No problem," Darlene replied, shoving her purse under the front counter.

Darlene had worked here for almost four years. Maria was a good boss. She always treated Darlene with respect and even gave her an entire month off after her father passed away three years ago. She was an older Native American woman with a bushy head of white hair that she barely cared enough to run a comb through. She wore large glasses that looked like they were from the seventies. Her fashion left a lot to be desired. Maria seemed to put on whatever she grabbed first and didn't look twice in the mirror afterward. For instance, today she had on a blue shirt with an off-color green skirt and black shoes. Her earrings were painted octopuses she had probably made herself — she liked making crazy jewelry.

"So," Darlene asked. "What happened with Jacob?"

Maria scowled. "He comes into work high as a kite, stinking of weed. Starts rambling to me about how he was in the woods last night and *like, totally felt something, like, man*," Maria said, mimicking Jacob's slow tone. "He was an hour late on top of it. I can't have someone late, stinking of weed and scaring off the few customers I get each month… especially after the last incident."

"Yeah, that was a mess." Jacob had hit on one of their regular clients in such a crass manner that she had threatened never to return again.

"Anyway, thank you so much for covering. I'm going to head off now. One of the grandkids is having a birthday party. You'll be okay?"

Darlene cast a sarcastic glance around the empty bookstore. "Wow, I hope I can handle it."

Maria laughed and grabbed her purse, heading to the door before stopping. "Hey, how was your date?"

Darlene frowned. "A total mess."

"Sorry, love. Hang in there, okay?" Maria said before leaving.

Hang in there. Darlene sighed. She has been hanging in there for way too long. When was she going to get a grip on her own life again? She walked around the shop to make sure everything was in its proper place. Darlene knew it would be, of course. It wasn't as if they had a ton of customers come through.

Maria had the marketable books up front, which brought in some tourist traffic during the summer. The farther back in the store one went, the stranger the books became. Darlene ended up in the back again, like she always did. Maria kept the supernatural books back here — books about ghosts, werewolves, mermaids and all sorts of paranormal creatures. Darlene always felt drawn to these; she never knew why. As a kid, she liked to pretend to be a ghost hunter. Nowadays, she liked to watch terrible B-movies about ghosts.

She trailed her fingers along the spines, letting the musty old-book smell wash over her. Darlene stopped in front of one book about ghosts, pulling it off the shelf. She had just flipped it open to a random page when the tiny bell on the door jingled. Surprised, Darlene looked up.

A tall man in amazing shape walked in. He had brown eyes, a beard and scruffy hair and wore a leather jacket. Darlene found herself gawking at him. He was so handsome her knees turned to jelly.

"Hi!" she said, but her voice sounded too high pitched, like she was eleven. "Hi, sorry, back here." She walked up front to him.

"Hello," he said in a deep voice that sent shivers down her back.

"Hi," Darlene repeated and then tried to get a hold of herself. "How can I help you?"

"I'm lost. I'm trying to find *Roman's Tavern*."

Her eyes widened. "I don't know if it's open yet."

Was this guy a hardcore alcoholic? It was still early in the morning, and he wanted to find a bar. *Roman's Tavern* was the only bar in town that Darlene hadn't ever gone to. It brought in a wild crowd that made her uneasy. Any time she drove past it and saw the crazy partying in there, she realized how much she wanted to go and that scared her. She was never much of a partier. The fact that such an overwhelming urge to go when she drove by made her nervous. What if she went and lost her head?

The cops were there often, breaking up fights. Bike gangs were always seen there. Sometimes, if she left work at closing time, she'd drive by it and hear the thumping music and smell the cigarette smoke. She thought about going in every time. What would happen? Would she get hurt? What if she was missing out on something?

To Darlene, *Roman's Tavern* represented a life she could jump into if only she wasn't afraid. But she *was* too afraid. Life as a hermit was too comforting.

"Do you know where I can find it anyway?" he asked.

"It's down the street. On the corner, kind of pushed back a bit. It has this rundown broken sign that you might see if you drive by it."

"Thanks a lot, Miss…"

"Darlene." She held out her hand.

He stared at it for a second and then shook it. "Idris. Thanks for the help. You guys sell books about ghosts?" He pointed to the book she was holding when he came in.

His hand was so warm that Darlene had to snap herself back to the conversation. Was he sick? Shouldn't he be resting instead of going to some bar?

"Yes," she managed to respond. "We have a supernatural section in the back. Ghosts, vampires, werewolves…the usual."

"Werewolves, huh?" he replied. "Okay, well, nice to meet you."

Before Darlene could say anything else, he was gone.

She stood there, clutching her book to her chest, thinking about the feeling of warmth from his hand. What in the world was that about?

Chapter Two

Idris stopped in front of *Roman's Tavern*. It was located so far back from the road that it was easy to miss during the day. But he knew exactly how to get to *Roman's Tavern* — he had been there tons of times before he left town. Today though, something had pulled him toward the bookstore and before he knew it, he was standing in front of the cute and friendly girl who worked there. In his old life, he would have shamelessly hit on her. But that was before everything changed. Instead, he lied and said he had gotten lost and needed directions.

He took a deep breath and walked toward the entrance of *Roman's Tavern*. This bar was the local haunt in town for anyone who fell in the "paranormal" group, as Darlene would have called it. Idris had stopped coming to places like this. They made him feel out of control and he hated it. He loathed anything that made him remember what he was — a werewolf. If he could have, he would have lived in seclusion, but no one would let him do what he wanted. Now he was being dragged into yet another scuffle between the pack here in Waterfall Grove and his own pack in Hedge Hills.

The door opened with a creak. Roman, the leader of the pack here, owned the bar and had a place to crash upstairs. His girlfriend often kicked him out due to their constant and vicious fights, but they never broke up. Idris knew he'd be here. The bar looked terrible in the daylight. The floors were dirty, and it smelled of old cigarettes and booze. Occasionally, vampires would come into the tavern, but only if they were craving a fight. This bar was a werewolf haunt.

Mark, Roman's second-in-command, rounded the corner as soon as Idris entered. He had a missing eye from a vicious fight with Roman six years ago, when Roman was vying for pack leader. Mark bowed to Roman after that fight and agreed to drop his claim.

"What the hell are you doing here?" Mark hissed.

"I need to speak to Roman," Idris replied, skipping the pleasantries.

"Roman doesn't want to speak to you or anyone else from your shitty pack," Mark said, crossing his arms.

This was what Idris hated the most. The stupid pissing contests between the packs. It all felt so childish. It reminded him of being ten years old and fighting with his friends at the playground. In the end, all of this amounted to absolutely nothing. Idris' patience began to wear thin.

"I need to speak to him," he repeated.

Mark scowled. "Are you deaf? You're not going to speak to him."

Idris took two steps forward, inches away from Mark's face, trying to control the urge to Change right in front of him and tear his throat out. "You are going to let me talk to him right now, do you understand? Or I'll leave you dead on the floor of this shitty fucking bar."

Mark shrugged. "Have it your way for now. Whatever has your panties in a twist isn't our problem." He moved to the side and avoided looking at Idris again.

Idris wasn't surprised that Mark backed down, given their history. There was no one in this entire area who didn't know about them. And now he had used fear to get what he wanted instead of taking the time to try to act like a normal human being. *But you're not a normal human being.*

Idris took a metal staircase in the back up to the top. The bar's second level overlooked the dance floor and offered a lot of dark corners where people could make out and drink. Idris opened a door off to the side, stepping into the offices and the one room that made up Roman's makeshift bedroom.

"Roman?" Idris called out.

There was a grunting noise of surprise and then Roman stuck his head out of the office, looking down the hallway. He was an incredibly large man, with scars down his cheeks from scratches from other werewolves. Roman had scars and marks all over from head to toe, from all the battles he had gotten into. He looked like a gladiator from ancient times. His hair was messy and sticking out at different angles. He had a jacket pulled on tightly but it looked as if his shoulders were going to pop right out of it.

"What the hell are you doing here?" Roman asked, echoing what Mark had already barked at him.

"I need to talk to you."

"Mark let you by? You didn't kill him, did you?"

Idris ignored the jab and tried not to let it get to him. "He let me by."

Roman looked him up and down, as if debating if he wanted to push this into a fight or just talk and get rid of Idris quickly. "Come in here."

Idris walked into the neatly organized office. There was no way that Roman put this together himself.

"Where's Julie?" Idris asked, trying to see if Julie had kicked him out again.

Roman shrugged. "I'm staying here tonight."

So she had. That explained his downtrodden spirit. Normally whenever Idris had to deal with Roman, it went as well as teaching a cat how to swim. Idris sat down across from Roman at his desk.

"Why are you here?" Roman asked, leaning back in his chair.

"The pack sent me," Idris replied. "Lucian has gone missing."

Roman's bushy eyebrows shot up. "Your pack leader is missing?"

"Yes, that's right. You're the closest pack. I wanted to know if you saw him pass through here."

"No, I haven't seen that son of a bitch pass through here. If he had, you'd know about it. He'd be dead up front in the bar."

"Charming," Idris replied dryly. "You have anything you can give me besides threats of what you'd do to a missing man?"

"When he go missin'?"

"Four days ago. Was leaving his shop and never came home." Idris glossed over most of the details.

Roman shrugged. "Haven't seen him."

"Nothing you can tell me?"

"You calling me a liar, boy?"

Breathe in, breathe out. Idris tried to control the urge to Change. "No. Roman, I am not calling you a liar. I am just trying to see if you happen to know anything."

"Well, I don't. And I don't appreciate you coming in here accusing me of knowin' something." Roman was getting angry now, having found an outlet for his anger about Julie.

Idris stood up. "I'm not accusing you of anything. Don't be pissed off at me because Julie kicked you out again."

Roman stood up as well, growling. "How do we know that you didn't do it?"

"Excuse me?"

"You! We all know you used to kill anything that moved. You tricked everyone into thinking you were fine and recovered, but what if you snapped and killed the pack leader to get his spot?"

Idris started counting to ten in his head in order to stop himself from reaching across the desk and dragging Roman over it. He was different now. He had to keep telling himself that.

"I'm done with this," Idris said, turning around.

"You are done speaking to me when I say you are, pup," Roman growled. "You're in my land now, not back at home."

Idris ignored him, leaving the office. He waited for Roman to burst through the door to attack him but there was nothing. Just like he had thought — a bunch of bravado. Still no closer to the truth about what had happened to Lucian. As Idris walked out of the bar, he thought at least he had kept his promise to himself — he didn't hurt any of the other werewolves, even if they did piss him off.

<<◇>>

Darlene came home and plopped her purse on the floor. She turned the oven on to heat up a pizza. Her social interaction with the one lone person who had come into the bookshop was quite enough for her, thank you. It was funny, most of the time when a customer came in, it felt like there was a glaring spotlight on her size. But Idris made her forget all about her size during their brief conversation. If only all conversations could be like that.

She wandered off to her computer, sitting down in the chair and staring out the window next to it. After Idris left, she had idly flicked through books about ghosts for the rest of the shift. Darlene couldn't help but think about *Roman's Tavern*. The man didn't seem like some sort of booze hound. And his hand was so warm! He was tall and built like a tank. She normally didn't like guys like that but she found herself drifting off thinking about him the rest of the day.

Darlene would have remembered a guy like that if she'd ever seen him before. He must have been passing through town. She wondered how long he was going to stay. Why was she thinking about this guy so much? She rubbed her eyes, sighing a bit, before booting up her computer. Darlene typed *Roman's Tavern* into the search bar and watched the results pop up.

The first was where it was located on the map, along with its rating. It wasn't rated that hot. She flicked through the reviews quickly.

"Everyone seemed to glare at me in unison when I came in..."

"Fight broke out while I was there and the guy walked out with a broken nose…"

"Dirty floors that looked like dog fur was the main décor…"

"The regular crowd here seems a little rough for my taste."

"Drinks sucked!"

Darlene went back to the search results page, staring at it. Why was she even looking this up? What was she looking for? She clicked on the homepage for the bar and found herself staring at some website that looked straight out of the 90s back when Geocities was still a thing. She expected to hear MIDI music start to play. Was there *clip art* on this page?

The main page said the bar offered a *well stocked bar as well as busy dance floor. Second story offers great places for low-key conversations.* Somehow she doubted that. The address was wrong, and there was no phone number on the main page. Darlene clicked through more of the pages but almost all of them were dead links. One page said *Roman's Tavern* was better suited for locals instead of tourists. It seemed an odd thing to write on their page. Darlene got a vibe that this place only wanted a certain group of people as patrons… even less of a reason for her to go try it out then.

She went through a few more pages of search results but they got less relevant as she went on. Darlene paused at one that caught her eye though —

Roman's Tavern theory? She clicked on it and it loaded a post from user 'SunnyWerewolf' from five years ago on an old message board labeled *The Dark Side of Night*, whatever the hell that meant. Darlene read the post:

Went here finally from the tip of user XOreal. What a trip! It was a terrible bar and I didn't see anything supernatural about it at all, honestly. I got there around eleven pm and it was packed but mostly by regulars. When I got inside it was like everyone began to glare at me all at once. The rumor was this place had some sort of supernatural vibe to it, like vampires or faeries or something, but it was just a bunch of pissed-off bikers acting superior to anyone who wasn't a local. I have always identified as a werewolf and was saddened to see I wouldn't be meeting any of my kin here!

Identified as a werewolf? Darlene felt out of her element. People identified as mythical creatures? She read the replies to the post but most of them were generic. There was one final reply though, six months after the original post. All it said was: *Come on a full moon.*

There was no reply. Out of curiosity, Darlene brought up SunnyWerewolf's profile. His post about the tavern had been the final post he ever made. She searched his name on the board and got a couple of other posts popping up, all about him.

Anyone heard from SunnyWerewolf lately?

Hey, whatever happened to SunnyWerewolf?

I guess he must have moved on to another board.

Darlene thought about the final reply to his post. The user who had made it had no other posts. It looked as if that reply to SunnyWerewolf was the only reason that account was created.

On a hunch, Darlene opened a new search window. She was acting ridiculous, of course. She remembered a murder that happened in town a while ago. The body had been found in the hills, maimed by wolves. The police never figured out why the guy wandered into the hills near the town. They were dangerous and ended in cliffs that could send a person who was not paying attention over into the ocean. Darlene's imagination always ran wild at night. When it did, she usually went on some online game and talked to strangers — no one minded a person acting odd online. But she started typing into the search bar instead.

Old articles about the case popped up. Five years ago. She flicked back between the post telling him to come on a full moon and when SunnyWerewolf had gone missing. The dates synced up. SunnyWerewolf had gone missing on the full moon and was last seen at *Roman's Tavern.*

Had the police known about this post? The case was concluded as a drunken accident but what if they had never seen this before? Darlene's heart began to beat very quickly. She couldn't just ignore this. What if there was a link? Did the person who posted, asking SunnyWerewolf to come to *Roman's Tavern,* kill him and make it look like an accident?

Darlene exited the browser windows quickly, as if they suddenly had eyes watching her.

21

Chapter Three

Idris walked into the police station when he saw Darlene from the bookstore being led out of the back office with a detective. She looked upset and frustrated. Understandable, Idris thought, since she had just been talking to cops. He didn't want to be here either, but he wasn't able to pick up Lucian's scent at all. At least if he filed a missing persons report, he'd be notified if someone found him.

As he walked up to the main desk, Darlene spoke to the detective. "You don't find it curious he believed he was a werewolf and vanished on a full moon?"

The detective mumbled something non-committal, with an expression that said he was sick of talking about it. But Idris froze. Why was she talking about that old case? He knew it was that because she mentioned that guy who thought he was a werewolf. Brent had shown up one night to *Roman's Tavern*, rubbing everyone the wrong way, claiming he was a werewolf looking for a pack. He wasn't a werewolf. Idris happened to be there that night, back when he still ran with Roman's pack. He wanted to rip the kid apart for invading their spot, claiming to be one of them, when no one in their right mind would want to be one of them.

Brent left soon after, and Idris didn't see him again. But he turned up dead in the woods six months later, on the night of the full moon, when everyone was Changed. The cops ruled it a drunken accident, saying Brent had pissed off some wolves. But everyone knew better. The kid had been mauled by werewolves and left for dead in the woods. No one came forward to admit they had killed Brent. Roman blamed Idris, saying he had lost it and had wanted to kill the kid previously. That was when Idris broke free from the pack, which kicked off more trouble.

"Hello?"

The voice snapped Idris out of his memories. The assistant in front of him looked irritated — she probably said hello to him at least three times, judging by her tone.

"Sorry, excuse me." Idris turned around, following Darlene.

She left the police station and walked toward her car.

Idris jogged after her. "Excuse me?"

Darlene stopped and turned around. She was pretty. Her features were girlish with large, bright blue eyes and chestnut brown hair swept back out of her face. Everyone in his pack used to make fun of him for his penchant of falling for bigger girls who ended up breaking his heart, probably because he used to be an ass and deserved it, but Idris ignored the teasing. He always liked his girls on the thicker side and was proud of it. Darlene fit into that box nicely.

"Oh, hi, Mr. Idris," Darlene said, blinking those pretty blue eyes at him. "Did you find *Roman's Tavern*?"

"Yes, thank you," Idris replied. "I couldn't help but overhear you mentioning the murder that happened a few years ago."

Her face fell. "Yeah, I thought I found something new to the case but they weren't interested." She shrugged. "How did you know what I was talking about?"

Idris wasn't sure how to lie properly to her without mentioning the tiny little fact that it all had to do with werewolves. "To be honest, my friend just went missing. Seemed like a long shot but someone mentioning an old case like that at the same time my friend went missing…" He trailed off, but realized it was true — that was why he came after her, wasn't it?

"Your friend is missing? I'm really sorry to hear that," she exclaimed. "Is that why you were checking out that bar yesterday?"

Idris nodded. "Yes, I was checking to see if he passed through. No luck though."

"Yeah, I just…I found this post online telling the kid — I guess his name was Brent but he posted as SunnyWerewolf — to come to that bar on a full moon. And then he vanished. What if the police didn't know about the post? Someone telling Brent to come back to the bar and then he vanishes and shows up dead, you know?"

Idris' heart started beating very hard. There was a *post* telling Brent to come back to the bar? He didn't know about that. The case suddenly burst wide open in front of him. After everyone had denied responsibility for it and tried to pin it on Idris, no one seemed that interested in finding out the truth. But now…

Darlene's phone suddenly rang and she looked down at it. "Oh, this is my best friend. I've been blowing her off lately. I have to take this or she'll kill me."

"I understand," Idris said. "When do you work again? I'd like to hear more about what you found about Brent."

"That was mostly it. The police blew me off. Said the case was closed and a post wasn't enough to warrant opening it up again. But I start work tomorrow at ten in the morning." She looked down at her phone. "Okay, I'll see you later!"

Darlene answered the phone, turned around and walked off. Idris caught himself staring at her bottom as she walked away. He shook his head before returning to make the report about Lucian. As he walked into the police station again, Idris wondered — what was Darlene doing that made her find that post in the first place?

<<<>>>

"Why are you vanishing again?" Rebecca demanded when Darlene answered the phone. "Every time I try to pull you out of the hole, you're back in real life for about two weeks and then you go back to being a hermit," Rebecca said loudly into her phone as Darlene sighed. "Was it that terrible date you went on?"

"I'm trying. You know I am," Darlene replied.

"You know I love you, Darlene," Rebecca said after a long pause. "But you can't keep letting what happened with Austin hold you back from living. I'm not sure how else I can help you except by telling you the truth. You need to find a way to move on with your life and stop living by yourself and closing everyone out."

After Darlene hung up, she returned home and curled up on the couch, with a bowl full of ice cream and some terrible reality show about gypsy brides who loved toddler beauty pageants or something. She had known Rebecca for over ten years now. They met online before they realized they lived only thirty minutes from each other. Rebecca lived in Hedge Hills and often wanted to see Darlene. They used to see each other all the time back when Darlene was dating Austin. But everything went to hell, and she hadn't seen Rebecca in over six months.

Rebecca meant well and wanted Darlene to get better and to get her life together. But Rebecca had a good job and a steady boyfriend. Rebecca was adorable and chubby in a way that guys didn't mind, unlike how Darlene felt about herself. Rebecca didn't think Darlene was trying to get better. And to be honest, Darlene didn't think she was trying to get better either.

She didn't know how to move on after losing Austin. They had been together for five years and she loved him every second of the day, more fiercely than the last second. Austin was tall, blond and handsome. He made Darlene feel as if she was the most beautiful woman on the entire planet. They used to spend time reading books together or laying by the pool of his parent's house, letting the sun cook them as they sipped cocktails. It had all been amazing.

And then Austin proposed. The ring was enormous. Austin had been saving up for it since their first date because he knew she was the one. Life couldn't have been better.

Darlene tried to shut the thoughts down before they came back in full force. She did herself no favors when they did and ended up drinking. Rebecca meant well by her tough love talk but it just depressed Darlene. She pulled her blankets tighter around herself and thought about how the police officer had blown her off completely with her information about Brent aka SunnyWerewolf. He told her the case was shut and had been solved for quite some time and not to be playing detective at home.

It pissed her off. She wasn't playing detective at home. Darlene was still bothered by the post. And then Idris showing up…

He said his friend was missing. The first place Idris looked for his friend was *Roman's Tavern*. It just seemed odd to Darlene that Brent had gone missing there and Idris checked there first. And now Idris was going to stop by to see her again to talk about what she knew about Brent.

That was another thing that Darlene didn't want to think about. When she was actually talking to Idris, she didn't feel self-conscious at all. Idris was gorgeous in a rugged way. But she couldn't just walk away when someone started a conversation with her. She was terrible with people but not *rude*.

There was just too much social interaction for Darlene today. She wanted nothing more than to cover her head with the blankets and ignore everything going on in her life.

The next day, Maria held interviews to replace Jacob so Darlene watched the front shop. There were no customers, as usual. The applicants who came in were college kids looking for a part-time job or tiny, little old ladies looking for something to do. Darlene didn't care who Maria hired. They never needed two people to man the store at one time. The best employees were the ones Darlene never had to hear about, unlike Jacob, whom she only met once and felt as if she knew him like a brother from how often he had messed up.

Darlene was idly flipping through a book about werewolves when the front door chimed. She looked up and saw Idris walk into the bookstore. He looked tired, with bags under his eyes. His jacket was zipped up tightly but Darlene could still see the muscles rippling beneath. His hair was messy, and stubble graced his chin. His eyes were a dark gray, like storm clouds. Darlene tried to ignore the butterflies in her stomach.

"Hey," he said, walking over to her.

"Hi," she replied, hoping her tone was casual. "How are you?"

"I'm good. Tired."

"How did the police report go?"

His gaze fell on the book in front of her. "What are you reading?"

"Oh!" Darlene looked down at the book. "It's called *The Werewolf Code*. Just…it's silly…I like reading in that section…you know. Um, I find it interesting to read about things that probably aren't around us. I said probably, I meant — not at all. No one is like that. I…" She trailed off, mortified with how much she was rambling on to him.

"I've read it," Idris admitted.

"Really? You've read *The Werewolf Code*? That's great —"

"Who's this?"

Darlene turned around to see Maria come from the back office and look Idris up and down. "Oh, Maria."

"Somehow I don't think this is the next person I am supposed to interview — Mabel Rodgers."

"I'm Idris," he said, holding his hand to Maria. "Darlene's friend."

Maria's eyebrows shot up. "Darlene's friend, really?" She glanced over at Darlene with an expression that said *I hope you tell me about this later*. "Nice to meet you." She shook his hand.

"I was just talking to Darlene about *The Werewolf Code*."

"Oh," Maria sighed. "Darlene just loves all that paranormal stuff. Especially ghosts. You into that stuff, too?"

"It's interesting," Idris replied.

"Glad you found someone else interested in that stuff, Darlene," Maria turned to head back to the office. "Let me know when the next person gets here."

Idris looked at Darlene. "The cops filed the report but they haven't seen anyone matching my friend's description."

Darlene sighed. "I'm sorry. That sucks."

"I was wondering about the post you found online," Idris said.

"Oh, yeah." Darlene pulled out her phone. "I found it last night on here to show you."

Idris looked down at Darlene's phone. He'd been surprised to find her looking through *The Werewolf Code* or that there was even a copy here. Idris hadn't seen a copy of that book in a long time. Every pack leader had one and gave it to anyone who had been turned. Idris remembered after the first time he Changed he spent a full week going through the book page by page, trying to find a way to reverse the curse. Idris couldn't find one, and he never looked at it again.

But there were only so many copies of the book in existence — one for each pack that had been together since the Dawn of the Change. If a pack didn't have a copy of the book then they'd reach out to share one from a friendly pack. The fact there was one just sitting here concerned him. He wanted to ask when the book was acquired.

Nothing about the post on Darlene's phone seemed to have come from anyone he knew. But there was the proof, staring at him right in the face, that someone had lured Brent back to *Roman's Tavern* to murder him.

"I don't know much about computers," Idris said, looking up at Darlene. "Is there any way we could track this?"

"That was the only post by that user. It looks like the account was created just to post that."

Idris looked back down at it, frowning. "Strange."

"Did the same thing happen to your friend? Did he think he was a werewolf, too?"

Idris wanted to laugh, but knew he couldn't. Lucian was a good pack leader, tough when he needed to be and knew when to bend to make sure the pack saw him as fair. His wife, Liara, was also a werewolf and was beloved by almost everyone in the pack for her gentle nature, even when they all had naturally violent sides. She cried so hard over Lucian going missing that Idris worried about drowning in her tears.

"No," Idris replied. "How did you get this book, by chance?" He pointed to *The Werewolf Code*.

Darlene looked at the cover, running her fingers over it. "Someone sold it to us, actually. About a month ago."

"Really? Did you see the guy?" Idris pressed, knowing he didn't sound casual at all but not caring.

"He was tall and wearing a suit. Although I remember the suit didn't fit properly. I notice weird things like that." Darlene shrugged, and Idris tried to ignore his desire to flirt with her yet again. She crinkled her nose when she was nervous, and it was adorable. "Anyway, he had glasses on with large frames. And he had this cellphone that looked like it was from the late nineties. A relic. He could have donated that instead. Anyway, he said he had this laying around and it took up too much room so he dropped it off here. Said someone would come by for it one day."

Idris felt numb all over. *Lucian*, Idris realized with a jolt. *Lucian was here and dropped the book off.*

"And that was it," Darlene finished. "Been sitting on the shelf just gathering dust. I mean, it is a huge book. I started looking at it and it's like…rules for being a werewolf and stuff."

"Can I see it?" Idris asked stiffly.

Darlene slid it over to him. At that moment, a woman who looked roughly a thousand years old, came into the bookstore. Probably Mabel Rodgers for her interview. Darlene excused herself to help the visitor. She walked with a cane and took a long time to cross the store. She had an open umbrella as well, which she seemed to be fighting to close. Idris thought the umbrella was weird, but old people were strange in general.

Idris turned back to the book. He opened the cover and checked the bottom of the first page. Lucian's initials were there. Idris' head felt light for a moment. This was his own pack's book. Why did Lucian disguise himself and drop it off here? *Said someone would come by for it one day, but who?* Idris trailed his fingers over the initials. Did Lucian mean Idris?

"Yes, right through here," Darlene said to the tiny old lady. "Maria, this is Mabel — okay, thank you." She shut Maria's office door with a soft click and let out a sigh.

As she walked back over to him, Idris looked up. "How much is this?"

"Let me look. No one has even asked before." She went over to the computer on the front desk, typing quickly before stopping. "$2,000."

Idris' eyebrows shot up. What was Lucian thinking? If he meant for Idris to find this, did he forget Idris wasn't exactly rolling in money? Darlene was looking at Idris patiently. He found himself admiring her blue eyes again before shaking his head.

"I want to buy it," Idris said. "But I don't have that sort of cash on me."

"You want to buy it?" Darlene replied, surprised.

Idris nodded, trying to come up with an excuse. "Yes, it looks interesting."

The way Darlene was looking at him made him nervous. There was no way she was going to buy any excuse he gave her. But he couldn't tell her the truth either. No one was supposed to know about the packs if they weren't one of them.

"Books that much are usually bought by high-end collectors. That's why they don't mind the price. It's not for casual reading."

"You can't wiggle on the price?"

Darlene shook her head. "Sorry, Idris. We're barely breaking even as it is. I don't know why Maria paid so much for it."

Idris found that curious but knew he hit his question limit for the time being. "Well, if she changes her mind, can you call me?"

Darlene's big eyes blinked. "Oh, sure."

They pulled out their cellphones and exchanged numbers. Idris hurried from the bookstore, leaving with more questions than ever.

Chapter Four

Darlene was doing the last walkthrough of the night. It didn't really matter, but Maria liked knowing that everything was in its proper spot and Darlene didn't like lying. As she slid *The Werewolf Code* back onto the shelf, she found herself thinking about Idris for the millionth time that hour alone. His phone number, now safely stored in her own phone, seemed to be burning a hole in her purse behind the counter. She knew he had given her his phone number for reasons other than any desire for her, but Darlene had never received another number from any guy since Austin — and that tragic date she was just on… but she liked to think that didn't count.

But Idris, no matter how good looking he was, was strange. His behavior seemed just off enough to make Darlene think he was hiding something major, not only about him but his missing friend, too. And his sudden desire to buy the book out of nowhere — one look inside told the reader that they were in for dry reading and a lot of strange jargon that made no sense.

Darlene's hand rested against the spine of the book. She took the book out again, balancing it with one hand then flipping it open with her other. The book was massive, at least 1,000 pages and had an old smell to it that was more than just that of a musty old book. She opened it to the first page, which was all Idris had looked at before suddenly deciding to buy it.

Darlene couldn't find anything out of the ordinary. Certainly nothing that screamed "Spend $2,000 on me!" She ran her fingers down the page idly, and saw something that wasn't part of the print. Initials — *LC*. Darlene suddenly knew that was why Idris wanted to buy it.

Darlene shoved the book back onto the shelf and went back to the computer. Maria stored data on everyone who sold any book to them for possible donations or sales in the future. She typed quickly and a page on the screen popped up about the book. The seller's name was *Luke Craig*. Without thinking twice, Darlene dialed the number to see if anyone picks up. It rang for almost a full minute.

"Hello?" The woman sounded as if she ate cigarettes for dinner.

"Hi, Luke Craig there?"

"No. Sorry, wrong number."

The woman hung up right away before Darlene could apologize for bothering her. So the phone number was fake. What did Idris know that he wasn't telling her? At least she knew he was lying now.

As Darlene was leaving, she thought that maybe it wasn't any of her business. Maybe she should just forget about it all together. Locking the front door of the bookshop, she thought about calling Rebecca to see if they could meet up. It would make her happy, and Darlene could use some social interaction that wasn't about missing people.

As she walked around the side of the building to the parking lot, she stopped for a moment. Maybe she was being paranoid, but she swore that she saw something dart away from her car. The parking lot was tiny and dimly lit. It was behind the building that housed not only the bookstore but the other two shops next to where she worked — the coffee shop and massage parlor. The massage parlor was closed for the night but the coffee shop usually stayed open until 10:00 pm. It must have just been someone from there leaving.

Darlene began to walk again, clutching her keys in between her fingers. Why was she getting such a sense of dread? Was it stupid to keep going to her car? She had a mental image of those bad horror movies when the person decides to investigate the source of the noise instead of running away as quickly as possible. Darlene stopped and turned around. She would figure something else out... like call a taxi. As she walked away from her car, she heard a noise. She turned around and saw a blur coming straight toward her.

The force sent her flying. Darlene shut her eyes to brace for the impact but then she felt steely fingers wrapping around her waist and slamming her against the back of the bookshop, out of sight from the coffee store. Darlene was out of breath and opened her eyes.

The woman who stood over her was deathly pale and had blood-red eyes. Darlene felt terrified just looking at her. Was this the same person who had just tossed her as though she was a ragdoll? There was no way. The woman had dark red hair tied up in a tight bun and was wearing baggy clothing that Darlene couldn't make out. Darlene tried to wiggle away but the woman's grip was iron tight.

"Where is he?" the woman asked in a low voice.

"What?" Darlene squeaked. How could this woman be so strong?

"Idris. Don't play dumb with me." The woman moved her face closer to Darlene's.

Darlene felt as if ice had been doused over her. *Idris.* She supposed she had made her vow not to get involved in people's business a little too late. The woman continued to stare at her with empty, emotionless eyes.

"He's not with me," Darlene said through shuddering gasps, unsure of what the woman was looking for.

"Where was he last?"

Darlene was unsure how to respond. Fear flowed through her veins, as if her entire body had been drained of blood.

"Answer me!" the woman shouted. "Or I'll make you my meal right now."

Darlene was going to squeak a response when suddenly the woman tilted her head back and fangs popped out. She hissed at Darlene.

"Oh my god," Darlene mumbled. "Are you a vampire?"

This just seemed to piss the woman off. She picked Darlene up again and threw her back against the wall. Darlene hit the ground and grunted, tasting the blood that filled up in her mouth. This was crazy. She had to be dreaming, right? Or did this woman have fake teeth in her mouth, because vampires aren't real —

"Tell me or I will kill you right now." The woman crouched down next to Darlene.

Darlene looked up at her. "Idris said he was leaving town and had found the trail of his friend back home."

Darlene held her breath. She hoped the woman believed her lie. Could vampires sense when someone was lying? It was as if all the useless knowledge that Darlene read about vampires suddenly slid out of her brain and landed on the ground next to her. She had no idea if her lie even matched up with what was going on, but if she could get the woman to leave, then Darlene could tell Idris what was going on.

"Did he take the book with him?" the woman asked.

"Yes," Darlene lied. "He took some big book with him. I don't know what it was."

The woman pulled on Darlene's hair and yanked her gaze to meet hers. "If you're lying, I'm going to come back and drain you. Do you understand? The only reason I'm not going to kill you tonight is because I'm feeling fucking generous." When Darlene didn't reply, she yanked on her hair again. "Say thank you!"

"Thank you," Darlene mumbled, her face blushing with embarrassment.

The woman let go of her hair and stood back up, looking down at Darlene in disgust. Then she glanced around the parking lot and ran off so fast that she was just a dark blur against the backdrop of the few cars still around. The blur jumped high in the air and disappeared over the rooftops.

Darlene just sat there and managed to prop herself up against the back wall. Her mouth tasted of blood and her entire body ached from the physical trauma. She slid her cellphone out of the jeans of her pocket. The screen was cracked but she was able to get it to turn on. Darlene brought up her contacts and hit Idris' name.

The hotel where Idris was staying at must be the worst in town. He wasn't entirely convinced that this wasn't just a front for some prostitution ring, because the turnaround rate on his floor alone was ridiculous. Half the time, he couldn't sleep because the moaning was so loud and fake that he wished he could Change into a bear instead to hibernate. Idris turned up the volume on the tiny TV in his room but the picture was so fuzzy he could barely make out what it was. It reminded him of when he was a teenager and would watch the fuzzy channels to try to find a breast. He was thinking about going to bed when his phone went off.

He didn't realize it was his own phone at first. No one ever called him. *Darlene*. His heart jumped up and lodged in his throat. He was trying not to think about her all night. Idris knew that Darlene had given him her number because of the missing people they had been discussing and nothing more. But he still found his thoughts drifting to her too often. He told himself that she probably just butt dialed him as he answered.

"Hello?"

A long pause of silence, and then finally Darlene's labored breathing on the other line. "Idris." Her voice was rough. "Bookshop."

"What's wrong?" Idris asked, standing up.

Another long pause filled with her ragged breathing as Idris grabbed his car keys and opened the door to the hallway. "Woman. Vampire." Idris' blood ran cold. "Please."

The call ended. Idris was already taking off down the hallway toward his car. The moon was high in the air, spilling light over the parking lot as he slid into his old pickup truck. Female vampire. Idris didn't even need to ask Darlene to describe her to him. He knew who it was. Vivica. And if Vivica was coming after Darlene, then whatever was going on just got a lot more serious.

It took him fifteen minutes to get through town to the bookshop. Idris pulled into the parking lot and saw Darlene's purse, the contents strewn about. Her car was still there. The coffee shop looked mostly empty and only had two other cars down at the end. Idris got out of his truck and looked around. Then he saw Darlene. She was sitting up against the back door of the bookshop, her eyes closed. Idris ran over to her, crouching by her side.

"Darlene?" he asked, afraid that Vivica had done something horrible to her.

Darlene's eyes fluttered for a moment and then she looked at him. "Hey."

"Are you bit?" Idris asked, running his hands over her arms to check for any bite marks before tilting her head to each side to check her neck.

"No," Darlene mumbled. "She said that would be for next time."

"We have to get you home, okay? You can tell me what happened later."

Darlene tried shaking her head. "Can't move. My body is so sore."

"I'll get you to my truck."

"No. I'm too big."

Idris ignored her and picked her up in one swoop. Darlene made a soft noise of surprise but Idris was already walking to his truck. He couldn't explain that his werewolf strength rendered almost anything light as a feather. He managed to get her into the passenger seat. Idris started the truck up, and the engine purred to life.

"Where do you live?" he asked.

Darlene managed to mumble out her address before she fell asleep. Her breathing was soft and slow, but as far as Idris could tell she wasn't wounded. He was sure that Vivica tossed her around enough to give her bruises that would last for days. Darlene only lived about ten minutes from the shop in an apartment complex that seemed a little rundown. The gate was broken and allowed anyone through, and there was a huge party in one of the apartments near the back.

Darlene's apartment was in a secluded spot, which was good because it meant no one would notice a giant man taking her into her apartment. With her keys in hand, Idris picked her up again and unlocked the door. The apartment was small yet incredibly clean. There was a bookshelf in one corner next to a computer and a couch with lots of blankets on it. The kitchen was neat and orderly. Idris could see her bedroom behind the kitchen. He walked to it and placed her down on her bed.

Idris shut the blinds, just in case Vivica was still around. He looked around and saw a dresser with little trinkets, tiny figures of things from different TV shows and a lamp. He flicked the lamp on and dim light filled her bedroom. There was a painting above her bed of cats playing poker, which he thought was cute. The night table next to her bed had a framed photo. Idris picked up the photo. It was a couple years old, Idris thought, because Darlene looked a bit smaller and her hair was long, swept up in a bun. She wore a pale pink dress that shimmered in the photo. She was smiling in a way that Idris had never seen before. And she was holding hands with an extremely thin man with messy blonde hair. He was tanned and had bright white teeth. He was holding her hand loosely and had a T-shirt on with khaki shorts. And they were both wearing matching rings.

Darlene was fast asleep now, her chest rising slowly. There was no ring on her finger now. He looked back down at the photo. Darlene looked so happy, her eyes shining and bright. The man next to her looked a little less excited, his eyes not bright at all and his grip on Darlene not as tight. *They must have broken up, although her having his picture right here isn't a good sign.* Idris put the picture back down. He knew all about broken hearts and old loves. It seemed Darlene had one of her own.

Darlene was running. She kept trying to run faster toward the church. But the storm clouds were rolling in, covering the church with rain and wind. The wind stopped her from making it to the entrance. She had to get into that church. There was a clap of thunder and Darlene looked over her shoulders. The graveyard behind her was growing darker and skeletons were rising from the graves. Their mouths were open as if they were trying to speak, but she didn't want to hear

them. Darlene turned back around and there was Austin on the church steps. The vampire had her arms wrapped around him, and she was biting into his neck, her red eyes flashing —

Darlene suddenly woke up and gasped for air. Sunlight spread in through the cracks in her blinds. She was in her room. Darlene tried to turn her head but her entire body ached and throbbed. Her mouth tasted faintly of blood. Her head pounded. She lay there, very still, trying to remember what happened. But the images seemed to twist with her nightmare, and she had a hard time remembering the truth.

"You're up."

Darlene painfully turned her head to the side and saw Idris in the doorway to her room. *Right* — she had managed to call him before the pain of being thrown around had become too much. He looked at her gently, his eyes soft in the morning light.

"Hey," she croaked.

Idris crouched next to the bed, uncapping a bottle of water. "I'm going to help you sit up for some water, okay?"

"Okay," Darlene croaked again, unable to find the energy to nod her head.

Idris managed to prop her up against the back of the bed but it was painful. Her entire body felt as if she had been hit by a car, especially in the front where Vivica had rammed into her. She thought of the stranger bearing down on her with those red eyes and it was as if she was taken back to that moment again. *Best not to think about it.* The water was cold and refreshing and before Darlene knew it she had drunk the entire bottle. Idris looked at her with concern in his eyes.

"How are you feeling?"

"Sore," Darlene replied. "All over. Thanks for getting me."

"Absolutely," Idris said. "As if I was going to ignore your phone call."

Silence filled the air and then Darlene cleared her throat. "I'll tell you what happened, but then I'd like to know exactly what is going on."

Idris nodded. Darlene wondered what he knew and if he was going to lie to her. He was clearly the reason that she was attacked. Darlene told her story, watching his face closely. He didn't seem puzzled by the description of the vampire who had attacked her, which made Darlene think he knew exactly who it was. He did seem surprised, however, when she mentioned that the creature had asked if he had taken the book with him when he left town. When Darlene finished, Idris was silent.

After a little bit, he finally spoke. "I need to look at the book, Darlene. *The Werewolf Code.* I need to know why Lucian sold it to you."

"The man who sold it to us is your missing friend?"

Idris nodded. "Whatever information he gave you..."

Darlene cut him off. "The phone number is fake. I already tried it. We can look up the address he gave though. And you can look at the book, but it has to be on the down low."

Idris held his head in his hands at this point and sighed. "I never meant for you to be dragged into this."

"Well, it's too late to freak out about that now," Darlene snapped, feeling irritated over the entire situation. "It's my fault, too. I shouldn't have looked into Brent. I should have just minded my own business. Now are you going to tell me what is going on or what?"

Idris looked up at her and chewed on his bottom lip, as if he was trying to think of what to tell her. Darlene suddenly felt afraid. This wasn't just going to be some run of the mill explanation. She still couldn't wrap her head around the fact that a *vampire* had attacked her.

"I'm not sure where to start," Idris finally said.

"Who attacked me?"

"Her name is Vivica. I've known her a long time."

"Is she really a vampire?"

There was a pause and then Idris replied, "Yes."

Darlene felt her head starting to throb again. "How can that be? How can she be a vampire? You're telling me they are real?"

"It's all real, Darlene. Vampires are real. Monsters you read about in legends are all real. They exist."

Darlene's vision went dim for a moment. This was way too much. She wanted to go back to bed. She pinched her skin on her arm and felt pain — no, she wasn't dreaming. She was awake for this insanity. The sad thing was she couldn't even tell Idris to stop being crazy. She had been attacked by Vivica herself.

"My friend Lucian has gone missing. And I'm trying to find him."

"Is Lucian a vampire, too?"

"No," Idris said. "He's a werewolf."

"A werewolf," Darlene repeated slowly.

Idris nodded. "He's a pack leader. I managed to trail him here. I was running cold until I heard you mention Brent. I thought the timing was funny, you know, about you mentioning someone killed by werewolves at the same time I was trying to find one."

"Brent was killed by werewolves? Was he one himself? He said online he was."

"No." Idris shook his head. "He wasn't. But I never saw that post you showed me of someone asking him to come back to *Roman's Tavern*." Darlene inferred from his tone that *Roman's Tavern* was a werewolf haunt after all. "Who lured him back to the club? Why was he killed? There are more questions than answers. And then you had a copy of *The Werewolf Code* that Lucian sold you — why did he sell you the book? Did he leave it there for me to find? Why did he run away?" Idris shrugged. "And now Vivica is involved, looking for me and the book. Vampires involved in werewolf affairs are never a good sign."

Darlene's breath came faster now as she looked Idris over. *Of course, he is so large and so warm and looks like he could tear someone in two if he felt like it. Idris is a werewolf, too.*

"I don't know what to do next. But if you're on Vivica's radar, that isn't a good sign. We have to get you out of town. Get you in a hideout somewhere… "

"Are you mental?" Darlene snapped. Idris looked at her in surprise. "If you think I'm skipping town and leave my entire life here to go hide out because of Vivica, you have gone mad. There is absolutely no way I'm leaving."

"Darlene, you don't understand. Vivica is going to come for you once she finds out that you lied to her. And now you know about werewolves and vampires. It's too risky. You have to get to a town with no packs or vampire nests."

"I'm not leaving." She crossed her arms, even though they ached and stared Idris down.

Idris stared back at her. "Why are you being so stubborn about this?"

"I'm sorry but you do not get to come into my life, rearrange it and mess it all up, tell me vampires and werewolves are real and then put me in…werewolf witness protection or whatever."

"What do you want to do then?"

"Let me help. I won't let you see the book unless I can help."

"And how are you going to help?" Idris shot back. "This is completely out of your element."

"Exactly. I'm your element of surprise."

Idris stood up. He was so mammoth that he seemed to take up her entire bedroom. He left the room. Darlene could hear him pacing in the living room, his big feet hitting the floor. She leaned back against the bed, closing her eyes. Her life might not be much but she wasn't going to run away. Darlene tried to imagine living in another town where no one knew her. No Maria, no bookshop, no Rebecca. Just…what? Her life almost how it was now minus the couple of things that kept her going. If Vivica wanted to take that away from her, then she'd go down with a fight.

Idris stared out the window of Darlene's room. The sun was high in the air. In the distance, children swam and jumped in the community pool, making a lot of splashes. Why was Darlene being so stubborn about this? Vivica could come back and kill her, but still she wanted to stay here and fight. Lucian had relocated others who stumbled across their secret. Idris never heard from them again and imagined they were living happy quiet lives. Not all the packs liked to do this. More than once, Roman had killed those who stumbled upon their secret or Changed them to get another member for the pack. Lucian never agreed on it. That was when the groups split off into two packs.

But Idris had never run into anyone who both didn't want to leave and didn't want to Change. Did Darlene just think she could live a normal life? No, because she said that she wanted to help him. What could a human do for him? Would she really not let him see *The Werewolf Code* unless he agreed?

Idris pulled away from the window and went back into Darlene's room. She had lay back down. Her skin was pale and bruises formed along her arms. She let out a grunt of pain when she turned to look at him.

"Here's the agreement. I don't want a human around me getting in the way," Idris said to Darlene. "But if you help me find anything useful in the book or some clue about Lucian, then we'll have an agreement. You can help me, and I won't try to get you to move away."

"Fine," Darlene agreed.

"No funny business, okay?"

"Fine." She shut her eyes before opening them again a moment later. "When do I have to worry about you changing into your werewolf form?"

Idris hadn't admitted to being a werewolf yet, but Darlene wasn't stupid enough not to pick up on it. "If I lose control of my emotion…or a full moon."

She nodded and before Idris could say anything else, she fell asleep.

Chapter Five

Maria grilled Darlene for a good twenty minutes about why she couldn't come in. By the time Darlene hung up her phone, she felt confident that Maria didn't believe one word out of her mouth. She debated texting Rebecca and saying hello, but she was unsure what to say. *Hey, Rebecca, got attacked by a vampire and now I'm trying to solve the case of the missing werewolf. Lunch next week?* In the end, she put her phone down and stared out the window of her bedroom for an hour, just thinking.

The thought of Vivica coming for her terrified her. But Darlene didn't want to run. She felt as if she had been doing a lot of that lately. She ran from Austin when she found out the truth. She ran from all her past friends and most of her family. And she ran from her life, becoming basically a shut-in who only went to work and spent the rest of her time online. It seemed silly to make a stand now, against a vampire who could kill her in one swipe, but it felt right to her.

Darlene was sick of thinking about Vivica. She had been trying to find something to give to Idris, some sort of clue that proved that she belonged on the case with him. The werewolf and the fat girl. *Don't. Don't start hating yourself right now.*

She stared at her laptop. Idris said he'd be back later to check up on her but didn't tell her where he was going. Darlene found herself wondering where to go first. She knew nothing about Lucian or *The Werewolf Code*, but she did know a little bit about Brent.

Darlene spent some time looking up things about him and tracking down his blog online where he talked about what it was like to be a werewolf. Idris confirmed he wasn't one and the blog made it clear he wasn't either. It was just entry after entry about struggling with being a werewolf that couldn't transform and how it was his "kin-type". Most of it went over her head. Brent struck her as a very sad guy who had just turned eighteen and seemed unsure of where to go in life.

She read post after post of Brent's struggles until she found the post that he made after he had gone to *Roman's Tavern* the first time.

Hi everybody. Going to Roman's Tavern was a bust. I heard it was a supernatural haunt in the area. I was excited about being accepted as a werewolf but it didn't go as planned at all. Some huge guy with bushy eyebrows jumped on me as soon as I told him I was a werewolf looking for a pack. He said I wasn't a werewolf and to stop trying to get attention. I was terrified because it looked like he was going to rip me apart. Some guy with glasses stopped him though, and I left soon after. The guy who saved me didn't give me either one of their names but thank the moon for him. I'm afraid he would have killed me on the spot!

Darlene jotted down some notes. *Guy with glasses — Lucian?* And was he stopping Idris from ripping this kid's throat out? She would have to ask him. Idris hadn't mentioned anything about being there the night that Brent showed up. She felt a cold sensation in her stomach — why didn't he tell her? The blog post didn't sound like Idris at all, but this was a long time ago. Who knew what happened to Idris since then?

Darlene went to Brent's final post of the blog. All it said was… *Wish me luck.* Darlene rubbed her eyes, tired. Where was the link? She had to be missing something. Who lured Brent back to *Roman's Tavern*? She searched for more, digging deeper until she found it — the name of Brent's mother.

It didn't take her long to find Brent's old address.

Idris felt as if a lot happened, but it led him nowhere. In fact, things just seemed to get worse now that he dragged Darlene into it. He couldn't believe how he just told her everything like that. If he ever found Lucian again, he would be in for a lecture from the ages. And since Darlene refused to leave and go into hiding, what would Lucian do?

Idris tried not to dwell on it. He took another sip of his coffee. He was at the coffee shop next door to the bookshop. Idris wanted to look at the book but knew that Darlene would have to be there to help look things up for him on the computer. His phone buzzed, and he looked down to see a text from Darlene: *I found Brent's address. Might be a lead. Also why didn't you tell me*

Idris sighed and pushed his phone away. The real
reason was that he was embarrassed by his behavior
that night. Lucian had stopped him from attacking
Brent. And then when Roman accused Idris of being the
one who murdered the kid months later, Idris had had
enough. He wasn't sure what hurt more — that his pack
leader thought he'd kill someone like that or that he was
so close to actually killing Brent the first night he had
come by. What if he had Changed and had no memory
of killing Brent? But that wasn't right, because Lucian
swore that they had been together that night. Idris
remembered that too, but was terrified he was just
making up memories that weren't real. Would Lucian
try to protect him like that?

Idris could remember them drinking and watching a
game at a bar nearby. Tensions had been high between
him, Lucian and Roman. Lucian didn't like how Roman
ruled the pack and was talking about leaving. But
leaving a pack was a serious thing and Roman wouldn't
take kindly to the threat of another pack close by.
Lucian was second in command at this point and was
trying to convince Idris to come with him.

Idris had been thinking about it, if only because his
behavior had been getting so out of control he was
concerned about his well-being. When he was around
Roman's pack, he seemed to become even more
worked up and would attack anyone who he thought
had insulted him. Leaving the pack meant he could
fully focus on gaining control of his werewolf side.

Lucian was unlike any werewolf he had ever met before — calm, collected and kind. Under Lucian's pack rule, Idris might have a shot at redeeming himself.

But Idris hadn't decided to leave until Brent showed up dead and Roman had blamed him. Upset at being blamed for the death of a kid pretending to be a werewolf, Idris agreed to break from the pack with Lucian.

It didn't go well.

Idris shook his head, dispersing the memories from his mind. He looked back at his phone. Going to talk to Brent's mother would be the next best thing, at least until Darlene returned to work tomorrow and he could look through the book. He picked up his phone and texted, *Sounds good. I'll come over now. I'll explain about that night, too.*

He paid for his coffee and left.

An hour later, Darlene was wedged in Idris' ancient pickup truck, bouncing along toward the highway. Each bounce of the truck sent dull throbs of pain along her body. She had some pain reliever pills on her and took a couple more.

"This truck is terrible," Darlene mumbled.

Idris glanced over at her. "It's a classic."

"That's what people say when something is old and crappy," Darlene grumbled.

She didn't mean to sound so grumpy but the last thing she felt like doing was driving an hour to go see Brent's mother. Darlene thought she'd have a day or two to figure out what they would say to her, but Idris wanted to leave right away. Darlene had agreed because she wanted to be there, too. Not that Idris was mean, but he was somewhat terrifying to look at if one didn't know he was a werewolf… which was something Darlene was still trying to wrap her head around. Werewolves, vampires…what else? Hopefully not zombies... she hated zombies.

Still, Idris is incredibly handsome and... she told herself to stop thinking because it was just going to lead her down a bad path.

"Why couldn't this wait?" Darlene asked.

"We only have two leads right now. Brent, which might not even be a lead, and whatever Lucian has in *The Werewolf Code*, which he shouldn't have gotten rid of anyway because only a true pack can have a copy. That means if anyone in my pack finds out Lucian got rid of the book or sees our copy is missing, we lose official pack status."

"Who revokes pack status?" Darlene asked. "Some werewolf council or something?"

"No. All the packs in the area vote in on major issues that affect all packs. That book lists absolutely everything you need to know about werewolves. It was originally started by the first pack and over the years other packs added to it until the version we have today.

The only other pack in the area is Roman's, and he's out for blood from our pack."

"Why?"

She could see Idris hesitate, as if he wasn't sure what to say or where to start.

"You said you were there the night Brent first went to the bar," Darlene prompted.

Idris nodded stiffly and then began to talk. His voice was low and throaty as he told her how Brent arrived at the bar that night, claiming he was a werewolf. As he told her about wanting to start a fight with Brent, Darlene could see the torment in his eyes.

"I used to be like that," he said to her. "All the time. I wanted to fight everyone. The Change…it pissed me off. When I got bitten, I was furious. I wanted to take on the entire world and make them pay for turning me into a…monster. I was vicious for ten years. Vicious, Darlene. I did things that are so shameful that I will carry that burden until the day I die."

Darlene didn't know what to say. She couldn't relate on that vicious level. After she lost Austin, all she had left was her sadness. There wasn't any rage left inside her. Idris spoke about Lucian, how he wanted the pack to be kinder and not terrorize people so much.

"But Roman loved being the only pack in the area. Like I said earlier, if there was an issue that affected the area, all the packs would discuss it. Being the only pack in the area meant Roman was a king, of sorts. When

Brent went missing and turned up dead by a werewolf, he blamed me… said I did it. But Lucian was there with me that night and he knew I hadn't. Roman tried to get the pack to go against me. That was when Lucian and I broke off to form our own pack."

"I'm sure that went well," Darlene said. "Seeing as Roman seems really levelheaded over things."

Idris cracked a smile, which made Darlene's heart flutter. "It didn't go well. The fighting was brutal. When it finally settled down, Roman and Lucian formed a truce. But the truce is barely holding together and now that Lucian is gone…" He trailed off, sighing.

Darlene looked out the window, seeing the trees whirl by as they kept driving. There was more to the story, Darlene could tell, but she didn't want to press it. She knew how it felt to want to keep things to herself. Everything with Austin felt that way.

"So, you sort of explained werewolves to me," Darlene changed the subject. "How do vampires come into play? You seem to know Vivica?"

Idris sighed again and glanced at a car passing him. "Do you think anyone else on this highway is talking about this stuff or do they all get to play the license plate game?" He shook his head. "Werewolves and vampires are a terrible mix. They were around before us and see us as a hindrance to how they are supposed to live. Vampires are excellent at keeping themselves out of any sort of human affairs. And if they happen to be caught, they just turn whoever found them either into a vampire or kill them. No sweat off their backs…do vampires sweat?" Idris seemed to pause, as if this had never struck him before.

"Why do they think you're a hindrance?"

"Most packs don't want to kill a bunch of humans or want to control the human race, like vampires do. We just want to co-exist. But the vampires think humans are weak and would be better either dead or one of them. It creates friction. Werewolf packs try to stay away from vampires altogether."

"But you know Vivica," Darlene stated.

"Yes. Yes, I know Vivica. But after I first Changed, I searched for vampires. I found their nest. I was hoping to upset them so much they'd kill me. They didn't. I met Vivica instead, and we had a very unhealthy relationship for a few years."

"You tried to kill yourself?" Darlene asked, her eyes wide.

Idris shrugged. "Mind if we talk about something else the rest of the way?"

Darlene nodded, looking Idris over slowly. A werewolf who hated it and had tried to have a vampire kill him, tormented by Brent and now the possibility of Lucian being gone... She turned back to face straight ahead. Even though Idris had asked for a change of subject, they didn't speak the rest of the way.

Chapter Six

The house where Brent lived was quiet and at the end of the street. The paint on it was faded and there were three flower pots out front, all containing dead flowers. The roof was dirty, and the grass was brown in some spots. There was an old-looking Dodge Neon in the driveway with chipped silver paint. Idris could hear a dog barking but he wasn't sure if it was from a few houses over or this one.

He looked at Darlene out of the corner of his eye. He had shared too much with her, and it was his own fault. He was falling for her, as much as he wanted to trick himself into thinking he wasn't. The only other person who had known about Vivica and him was Lucian. Relationships between werewolves and vampires were strictly forbidden. They had a sick, twisted relationship. Idris was sure that Vivica would be back for Darlene out of pure spite and nothing to do with Lucian. How did she know about the book and Lucian anyway?

Darlene was already getting out of the car. The bruises on her skin had faded a little but she still looked rough for wear. Maybe Idris should have waited like Darlene had suggested. Perhaps it wasn't a good idea to show up to someone's home, a giant man like him and a woman with bruises all over. He was going to tell

Darlene to stop but he was already getting to know certain movements she made — her walk told him she was on a mission.

Idris followed, admiring Darlene's behind before telling himself to stop being so distracted. She knocked on the door and they waited. Idris couldn't hear anything inside. Darlene waited another minute and then rang the doorbell. This time Idris could hear someone shuffling inside slowly toward the door. The door opened and Idris saw a tiny old woman, her hair going gray and her skin pale. She looked exhausted, as if she hadn't slept in years.

"Hello, my name is Darlene and this is my friend, Idris," Darlene said, extending her hand. "Are you Ms. Boots?"

The woman hesitated for a moment and then shook Darlene's hand, glancing mostly at Idris. "Yes. How can I help you?"

"I'm sorry to bother you," Darlene said, having clearly formed a plan that Idris hadn't bothered to come up with. "But we knew Brent online."

"Oh!" The woman's eyebrows shot up. "Please, please, come in."

Darlene glanced at Idris with a look that seemed to say *this is going better than I expected*. The two of them followed Ms. Boots into her house. It still looked as though Brent lived here. There were action figures on display on a table near the door and his shoes still by the front door. As Idris followed her to the living room, he saw a door down a hallway that had a werewolf poster on it. *Must be his room.* Idris wished he could go inside it.

Ms. Boots sat them down on a couch that smelled faintly of mothballs. An old cuckoo clock was ticking away in one corner. The TV looked old and the carpet faded. It was clear that they were tight on funds. A cat slept in one corner, purring softly. Idris felt depressed just being in the room. Darlene chatted about how adorable the house was, flattering Ms. Boots, who seemed to eat it up.

"It's so nice to meet Brent's friends. I was so concerned, you know. He spent so much time on his computer, and I never saw anyone he said he was talking to." Her hands began to flutter around her chest. "And then once he finished high school, he never left the house. He just loved his computer. You knew him a long time?"

Darlene nodded. "Yes. We both did. Brent said he had some things in his room for us, and we were going to meet up and trade them but then…so we decided to come up today to see if we could find them. If that's okay with you…?"

Ms. Boots nodded sadly, glancing again at Idris. "He…did he say anything about…leaving that night?"

It was directed to him, Idris realized. Maybe she thought since they were both guys he would have told him more. Idris shook his head. "No, ma'am."

"Brent was confused." She was speaking quickly now. "He thought he was a werewolf."

"Yes, he mentioned that," Idris said suddenly, deciding to go with whatever Ms. Boots said.

She nodded. "Okay, so you two know then. I think he latched onto that after his father passed away when he was twelve. Brent always kept to himself, you know? He liked to be alone a lot and once the Internet became popular…I should have watched him closer but I don't know much about computers. He told me he found other people who were werewolves, too." Ms. Boots shook her head. "Some group they had."

Darlene glanced at Idris, as if to urge him on and Idris cleared his throat. "Did he say anything about going to that bar?"

Ms. Boots looked up, her gaze slowly becoming more focused, "No. The first night he went, he paid for a taxi with his own savings. We fought. I told him he was being ridiculous to go someplace that said it was a werewolf haunt or whatever. I told him he wasn't one, and he was going to get hurt. I had never seen him so angry when he stormed out and left. I stayed up all night. I tried telling the police this, you know, but they didn't think the werewolf thing was important. But I think it is."

"Why?" Idris pressed gently.

"Because the next time he left, the night he died, someone picked him up. I didn't see too much of him in the car but it was a beat-up looking thing. And he had shaggy hair and glasses."

Idris felt as if the walls suddenly caved in on him. Shaggy hair and glasses? There was no way…no way…they weren't at the bar that night. They were at Lucian's place all night, watching TV and discussing Roman. How could Lucian pick Brent up?

Darlene, sensing Idris' sudden shock, took over. "Did you see anything else, Ms. Boots?"

She shook her head. "No, but I was screaming at him not to go. That I would…I would have to kick him out if he kept going to dangerous places like that. But Brent got in that car…" Ms. Boots went very still, as if she was fending off tears.

The room went silent. Darlene's big blue eyes darted between Idris and Ms. Boots but Idris wasn't sure that he could trust himself to say anything without grilling Ms. Boots with a million questions.

Darlene leaned forward and gently touched Ms. Boots' hand. "I'm sorry for your loss."

Ms. Boots looked up now at the two of them. "You two knew him. You knew he was a good kid, an honest kid who just seemed lost. I don't think something killed him in the woods. I think he was murdered. And I think that man had something to do with it. Please, believe me. The police thought I was crazy."

Darlene squeezed her hand. "I believe you."

Ms. Boots seemed to relax and nodded. "I haven't been in his room since the police came. I can't bring myself to…please, just take anything you need. Otherwise it will just sit there. Anything Brent wanted you to have or anything you want to remember him by."

Darlene stood up. "Thank you."

She walked by Idris and slipped her fingers through his, tugging him out of the room. The human contact made Idris' body feel hot all of a sudden. They walked down the hallway, past Ms. Boots' room, which looked as if she had moved into it. The sheets were thrown back in the bed and an old black and white TV was on by it, showing an old sitcom. Darlene looked down the hall and then at Idris.

"Was Lucian the one who picked him up?" she whispered.

Idris nodded, numbly, his fingers still wrapped around hers. "It sounds like it."

"What did you guys do that night?"

"We watched TV and drank. Talked about leaving the pack," Idris mumbled back. "I had so much to drink that night that I don't remember exact details, like what time he got there."

She chewed her bottom lip. "Let's look in his room."

Darlene turned to face Brent's door, her mind swirling. Had Lucian really picked Brent up on the night of his death? Was he the one who had told him to come to *Roman's Tavern* the night of the full moon? If Brent did everything by computer, like his mom claimed, then maybe they'd find a record of who contacted him off the site. The poster on the door was peeling off. If Ms. Boot's hadn't come in here in five years, then it truly would be untouched.

Darlene steeled herself, glancing back at Idris. She was aware of their hands touching. His body was hot to the touch, and his pupils were dilated. He looked extremely stressed out, as if it was all too much. She felt the same way, still trying to get used to werewolves and vampires and now this.

She opened the bedroom door slowly. It was pitch black in here. The blinds were tightly shut. Darlene flicked on the light switch. Dust swirled up into the air as the two of them stepped inside the room. The walls were plastered with posters of werewolves. A movie collection in one corner contained mostly supernatural films and old horror movies. There was a bed in one corner, still unmade, the covers thrown back as if Brent had gotten up in a hurry. A laptop was on a rundown-looking desk. Piles of clothes were on the floor and school books were strewn about the room. The air was musty and with each breath Darlene took, she could feel the dust fill her lungs.

Idris looked like a giant in a little boy's room. He looked around slowly. If they had expected something to jump out at them, then they were let down.

"You should look around his room. I'll check out his computer," Darlene said, going on a hunch that computers weren't exactly Idris' thing.

She could tell she was right by the relieved look on Idris' face as he nodded and turned to one corner of the room. Darlene slid onto the computer chair and booted up his laptop. It made a low noise, almost as if it was grinding awake. She imagined that it had been offline for five years, and she was thankful that it still booted up.

Brent hadn't password protected it, probably confident that his mom would have no idea what to do with a computer. The desktop showed a beach background and there were files over it. None of them caught her eye. She opened his web browser and went through his bookmarks. There was the forum he posted on as well as fan-fiction websites and a link to his blog. She found a page to his email and clicked it. It was still logged in.

Darlene told herself that the cops had gone through all of this stuff already, and it was silly to think she could find something they hadn't. But the fact that Lucian had picked Brent up that night…

Darlene cast a quick glance over to Idris, who was lost in thought and holding a stuffed werewolf animal. It would have been a funny sight if Darlene didn't know the pain he was in.

She looked back at the email. Spam, spam and more spam was in the inbox. She quickly went through to five years ago, when Brent was using his account.

Notifications on forum posts and his blog made up the chunk of the mail. Around the time he went missing, Darlene found an email from an address of 540w@springboard.com. She clicked it open and read the message.

Hi,

Glad to see you got my forum post. We met already, the night you came to Roman's Tavern. You should remember — we spoke briefly outside before you left. I have a proposition for you that will change your life. Can you come again on the night of the full moon?

Darlene frowned, lost in thought. Could this be from Lucian? She was going to ask Idris if he had seen Lucian talk to Brent outside the bar when he came over, holding a thin notebook.

"What?" Darlene asked.

"This book. Look." Idris opened it, and Darlene saw book pages rubbed onto the pages of the thin notebook. "This is from *The Book of the Ancients*."

"What's that?"

Idris looked annoyed that he had to explain when he was clearly onto something, "Think of it as *The Werewolf Code*, only for vampires."

"Okay," Darlene replied slowly. "And Brent had these pages how?"

Idris shook his head. "I don't know. He got them from someone, maybe? I don't know how a regular kid would get this stuff."

"Look at this," Darlene said, and Idris leaned over her to read the email.

He smelled faintly of cologne and body-wash. Warmth radiated off of him, and Darlene had a mental image of curling up and resting against his chest before she shook her head to clear herself of the fantasy.

"Did Lucian talk to this kid then? Why would Lucian pick Brent up the night of his murder? How did Brent get paper drawings of *The Book of the Ancients*? Did he answer this email?" His questions were rapid fire.

"Let me look," Darlene replied, clicking over to the *Sent* box and flicking through the emails there. "There it is," she said and pulled up Brent's reply.

Hey!

I'm super glad to hear from you. I did what you asked outside the bar the last time and managed to find a copy of that book you were asking about. I know you mentioned you couldn't show your face in that part of town. I broke in during the day when they were sleeping and managed to rub some pages on paper for you, but I couldn't steal the actual book. Way too heavy. Hope that is okay? So you're coming to get me on the full moon then? Glad it was you! When I got the message on the forum, I thought it was someone playing a trick on me. I know you said you'd contact me and not the

Darlene started to feel in way over her head. Every time she thought she had a handle on things, slowly accepting the fact vampires and werewolves were a thing, something seemed to spring right up to send her back fifty feet. Idris clenched his jaw, staring at the computer screen.

"Do you know where the vampire book is located?" Darlene asked gently.

Idris shook his head. "No," he replied gruffly. "But apparently Lucian did."

Darlene pulled out a flash drive. "I'm going to back up what I can from his documents and save it on here."

"I'll bring this book," Idris said, shoving the thin notebook into his jacket pocket.

Darlene managed to back up everything Brent had in his documents and shut down the laptop. On the way out, they saw Ms. Boot snoring gently on the couch, her chest rising and falling slowly. Darlene felt a pang of pity for her. As they left, Darlene's phone rang. Idris shut the front door while Darlene took the call. It was Maria.

"Hey," Darlene answered. "Was I supposed to work today?"

"No," Maria said, but her voice sounded a bit funny. "I just heard that Jacob is missing."

"Jacob as in…the one we just fired from the shop?"

Maria heaved a sigh. "That's the one… went missing last night. I figured you should know. Cops came by asking questions so they might ask you some since he worked with us."

"Thanks for the heads up," Darlene said before saying good-bye and hanging up.

Idris stood in front of the truck, looking at her curiously. "What happened?"

Darlene shrugged. "Jacob, this guy who worked at the shop and we had to fire for being terrible, has gone missing. Maria gave me a heads up that the cops might come by."

"Missing?" Idris replied, his brow furrowing together.

Darlene walked over to the passenger side of the truck with a sinking feeling in her stomach. She couldn't shake the fact that Jacob suddenly going missing wasn't just a strange coincidence.

Chapter Seven

Darlene woke up as they pulled into her apartment complex. She had fallen asleep in the truck. The sun was already sinking below the horizon. She hated how quickly it got dark in the winter. She yawned and looked over at Idris, who seemed lost in thought.

"Let me walk you up," he said.

Darlene nodded, still rubbing the sleep from her eyes.

She was thinking about Jacob. He had gone missing last night after Vivica had attacked her. Her body was still sore, but she was feeling a bit better. Did Vivica find Jacob after she tormented Darlene? Darlene rubbed her head, feeling her headache coming back. She took a step forward and realized that Idris was still by the truck.

"What is it?" Darlene asked.

Idris just shook his head, and Darlene fell silent. Abruptly, Idris dashed out of the truck without saying a word. She looked around, a growing sense of dread in her stomach. Her apartment was out of the way from the main set of units, having been added on later. The parking lot was empty and an old playground nearby creaked from a small breeze. *Idris must be paranoid, he just isn't thinking clearly.*

Suddenly a dark shape burst out of the nearest tree. There was a flash of red hair and all Darlene could think was *Vivica*! She closed her eyes and braced for the impact of Vivica steamrolling into her.

But instead there was a roar and a gust of wind. Darlene heard thrashing noises and opened her eyes. Her mouth dropped open. Vivica was dodging out of the way of a wolf…no…Idris. He had Changed. Darlene's head felt dizzy. How could that be Idris? The beast in front of her was hulking in size, his fur bristling and standing up on his back. He snarled at Vivica and the teeth that were exposed could have easily torn Darlene in half. Vivica backed up, her fangs exposed, her red hair loose and flowing around her shoulders. Her eyes were bright red and angry.

Idris snarled and lunged off his hind legs. Vivica was fast but not fast enough. The two blurred together and rolled across the pavement. Darlene could only stand there, frozen by fear and knowing even if she wasn't, there wasn't anything she could possibly do to help. Idris was suddenly kicked back hard. He slid across the pavement and in a flash, Vivica was by Darlene's side. Her red eyes blazed. "You little bitch!"

Then she was taken down again. Darlene shifted to the left to get out of the way as Idris tackled Vivica to the ground, his snarls filling the air. Once again, everything became a blur. It made her head hurt.

Darlene shut her eyes tightly, wishing it would all go away.

When she opened them, the mammoth creature that was Idris was still fighting Vivica. But Darlene saw something behind Vivica. She blinked and tried to look closer. Something transparent in the trees behind the apartment complex. Was that a… No. Darlene rubbed her eyes and when she looked again it was gone. No, she was simply going crazy.

Idris let out a snarl and suddenly his jaws clamped down on Vivica's wrist, yanking her down to the ground. She snarled back, yanking on her arm. There was no blood.

"Give us back the book!" Vivica cried. "Your friend said that you have it, Idris!"

"Oh no," Darlene breathed, realizing that she had thought Vivica had meant *The Werewolf Code*, not *The Book of the Ancients*. Shit.

Vivica heard Darlene, and her head snapped up. Idris saw that she was distracted, and he clamped down harder on her wrist and tugged her down to the ground, getting ready to rip her throat out. Darlene closed her eyes again, terrified. There was a grunt from Idris and then the wind whipped around her. Silence, except for Idris' labored breathing. Darlene didn't move.

Finally, someone spoke. "It's okay now."

Darlene's eyes fluttered open to see Idris standing in front of her. He tugged his jeans back on but was shirtless. He was cut like a rock, his muscles chiseled and his arms defined by pure muscle. She was going to open her mouth to speak but suddenly felt overwhelmed. The last thing she thought of was the glowing figure in the woods.

Idris watched Darlene sleep. Her chest rose and fell at a normal pace. He cursed himself. He had overwhelmed her. Given her too much to chew on and then Vivica turned up. She would have killed Darlene if he hadn't Changed. Seeing him in his altered form must have been too much for her. He rubbed his eyes. Everything that had happened was almost too much for him. He tried to backtrack.

From what Idris learned from Brent's computer, that night he had shown up at *Roman's Tavern*, he had a conversation with Lucian outside the bar. Idris tried to recall that night but he was a heavy drinker five years ago and his memory failed him. He could remember yelling at Brent, telling him to bugger off pretending he was a werewolf. Why did Brent even come up to them? Was it because of Lucian? He remembered wanting to fight Brent, but Lucian held him back and told Brent to leave. Lucian must have gone with Brent outside to talk to him. About what?

But Idris knew the answer to that… to steal *The Book of the Ancients*. But why did Lucian even need a copy of that book? The original was in some ruin somewhere, which meant that Brent found a copy of it among a vampire clan. He had broken in and transferred pages to the notebook. Idris pulled out the notebook and flipped through the pages. He couldn't read the language and didn't know what he was looking at. Frustrated, he let out a sigh and closed his eyes.

Vivica thought he had the book. Darlene must have lied and said Idris had it, meaning *The Werewolf Code*, but Vivica meant the vampire book. The whole thing made his head ache. He didn't understand any of it.

Darlene shifted and opened her eyes, mumbling his name. Idris went to her side, looking at her. Luckily, she remained untouched in the fight but must have passed out from shock. Idris helped her sit up and gave her water to sip. Darlene's big blue eyes looked at him, and Idris felt warm all over. What were these feelings that she brought up from inside of him? Lucian had been his mentor and it was as if everything he had known and loved about him crashed down around him and that made Idris want Darlene even more.

He did it without thinking. He leaned forward and kissed her. Darlene let out a soft gasp of surprise, but she kissed him back. A warmth that Idris had never felt before rolled through him. It wasn't the heat of being a werewolf. It was something more. Something deeper awakening inside of him. Idris backed away a little, tilting his face to look down at her. He wanted to make sure this was okay — that Darlene wanted this as much as he did. She nodded and that was all Idris needed.

His lips met hers again, and he kissed her. He wanted to kiss her hard and take her on the spot but he had to be gentle. He didn't want to hurt her because he knew she was still sore from Vivica throwing her around. He kissed along her neck and slid his hands down her sides. He liked the feel of her. She stiffened under his touch and not from the pain. *She's shy.* Was it because of her weight? How could he explain to her that the very thing she hated was the thing that made her so attractive to him?

"You're beautiful," he murmured gruffly into her ear.

"No," she breathed back, closing her eyes.

"Yes," he whispered, kissing down her neck.

"Guess this means I've earned the right to help you."

Idris smiled into her neck. "Guess so."

Idris wiggled his fingers up under her T-shirt, running his fingers along her belly. He loved how much of her there was. He felt himself harden in his jeans, almost painfully, as he ran his hands over her belly and down her sides, feeling her skin. His desire thrummed through him. Idris wanted her, all of her. Darlene looked up at him with those beautiful, big, blue eyes that were hazy with desire and he knew she wanted it as well.

Darlene felt her entire body quiver. She wasn't used to anyone looking at her the way Idris looked at her. She usually felt so shy over her size and how she looked, especially lying down, but Idris seemed only enflamed by desire when he slid her shirt over her head.

He went slowly and tenderly, knowing her body was still sore. Her face was hot with embarrassment — what if he didn't like her without her clothes on?

But with her shirt off, seeing her in her bra, he let out a soft moan. Darlene watched as he tugged his own shirt off. Once again, she saw those clearly cut and well-defined muscles. She ran her hands over his abs, marveling at them. Idris was so fit and well built. His body was so warm, like touching a fire. Darlene remembered what she had read about werewolves — how they ran hotter than humans and always felt warmer to the touch. Darlene loved it.

Idris leaned down and kissed down her neck again, toward her bra. He let out soft moans as his hands would slide over her skin and squeezed it. *He likes it, he likes that I'm a big woman.* This time, she let out her own sigh of pleasure as he tugged down her bra, exposing her breasts to the cool air. Idris immediately rolled his tongue over her nipples before taking one in his mouth and sucking and then switching to the other one. Knowing that Idris liked her body this big, she felt more confident and ran her hands along his back, mumbling his name.

His warm hands teased her breasts, slowly kneading them with his fingers, while he sucked on her nipples. She could feel how hard he got, pressing against his jeans. Darlene wanted more. Her hands traveled to his jeans and gave a tug. Idris read the signal and leaned back as Darlene unzipped his jeans and tugged down his boxers. His stiff manhood throbbed, and Darlene took delight in the size of it. She had never been with anyone this large before.

Idris watched Darlene as she stared at him lustily. He loved how full her breasts were and how luscious and large her body was. He couldn't wait anymore. He gently nudged Darlene back to lying down as he slid her own jeans off, followed by her panties. The smell of her brought out the animal in him and drove him mad with lust.

"I need you right now," he groaned.

"Take me," she whispered back.

That was all Idris needed. He positioned himself accordingly and slid into her. Her warmth engulfed him. Idris let out a moan of pleasure, louder than any of his other ones. Darlene murmured something and arched her back. Her hair spilled out across the pillow, and her blue eyes appeared hazy and dark in the moonlight. She looked beautiful and tonight she was all his.

Idris grunted and slid in more. She was tight and seemed to send her own warmth through his body. Finally he was fully inside her. Idris leaned over her and began to thrust. He started off slow, making sure she was okay. Holding back was agonizing. She let out small whimpers of pleasure, whispering his name. Her hands pressed against his back.

"More," she mumbled.

He thrust deeper into her. Darlene threw her head back and let out a moan. He was so large that it felt like he was filling her up. Darlene pulled him closer to her. Idris' body gave off so much heat that beads of sweat formed on her brow. Their bodies slicked up and slid together as Idris pulled all the way out and then pushed all the way back in. She moaned for him to do it harder and faster. Idris obliged. Waves of pleasure raced through her entire being. Her eyes shut as she clung to him, forgetting everything else besides Idris deep inside her. They moved together like this, perfectly in sync, for quite some time until finally Darlene's hips bucked. She was going to come. Darlene mumbled Idris' name before taking all of him inside her again.

"Oh!" she gasped in surprise as her orgasm broke through.

Waves of pleasure rippled through her core. She matched his thrusts, moving against him as hard as she could. Her hair stuck to her face from their sweat as she rode her orgasm through.

As Darlene came down from her own beautiful orgasm, Idris began his. He yelled out her name and thrust inside her, grunting. He held down her hips and spilled his seed inside her, his eyes tightly shut. He shook against her. His entire body formed rivulets of sweat as he finished his orgasm. After he came down from it, Idris slid out of Darlene and lay down next to her.

They both fell asleep in moments.

<<◇>>

The next morning, Darlene heard her alarm going off. She let out a groan. For the first time ever, she didn't feel like going to work. And why was it so hot in here? Darlene opened her eyes and for a second, the sight of Idris sleeping naked next to her didn't make any sense. And then it all came back. Last night. Their arms entwined. Idris kissing her. Having sex on her bed until late into the night. Darlene felt her face flush, and she closed her eyes. She was on the pill for birth control but she still couldn't believe she had slept with him. *Oh my god, what have I done?*

She hadn't been with anyone since Austin left her at the altar. The experience was so horrifying that Darlene had given up on life and was just going through the motions. To have the man she loved so deeply leave her — for a man, no less, not even another woman — had been enough to scar her till the end of her life.

Austin had been using her to cover up the fact that he couldn't be true to himself. He was gay and couldn't accept it. How many times had he thought to himself, *Darlene is fat and I'm doing her a favor*? She didn't know. After he left her at the altar, telling her that he was gay and couldn't go through with it, she had made sure never to reach out to talk to him again. She couldn't bear it.

On the other side of the bed, on the night table next to the sleeping Idris, was a framed photo of her and Austin. They had just gotten engaged when the photo was snapped. *Stupid, stupid, why am I thinking about this now?* She shouldn't be thinking of Austin anymore, but whenever she tried to throw the photo out, she couldn't bear it.

Darlene slid out of bed. Idris remained in a deep sleep, snoring loudly. She had to get to work. Idris didn't wake up during her morning routine of showering and changing. Before she left, Darlene hovered in the doorway of her room, watching Idris sleep. Should she wake him up? But Darlene didn't want to talk to him and have to discuss what they did last night. No. She shook her head and left her apartment, shutting the door softly behind her.

When Darlene parked her car at work, she saw that there was already a cop car in the parking lot. *Jacob.* In her lust for Idris, she had forgotten all about him suddenly vanishing. They must be here to question her. She took a deep breath and opened the door of the shop. Maria was chatting up the police officer, who was clutching a coffee from next door. He was laughing at whatever story Maria was telling.

As Darlene entered, Maria waved. "There you are. Officer Walsh stopped by to see you today… about Jacob."

Darlene walked over to him. He had a mustache that was too big for his face. His hair was slicked back and clearly dyed to hide the gray that was probably encroaching faster than he wanted. His eyes were wide and dark brown, and he gave Darlene a firm handshake. Cops always made Darlene nervous. Even when she did nothing wrong, she still felt nervous, as if they would arrest her on a whim.

"How can I help you, Mr. Walsh?" Darlene asked, hoping to sound like a proper adult.

"I'm sure you heard about Jacob Richardson. We're interviewing everyone who had contact with him recently, trying to gauge where he may have gone. I know he was recently let go from here."

Darlene nodded as Maria said, "Let me offer my office for you two to sit more comfortably."

Maria ushered them into her office and waved as she shut the door behind her, going back out front. Maria's office was decorated in all sorts of old Native American art she had collected from over the years. Officer Walsh sat on Maria's side, which Darlene found odd, almost as if she was interviewing for a job. She played with one of the blankets on the side of the chair she sat down on. Why didn't he just sit down on the couch next to her in the corner of the room? Could cops sit on couches with people? Why was she freaking out like this?

"This won't take long." He flipped open a tiny notebook. "Maria mentioned that with the schedules here, it didn't give you much of a chance to see Jacob."

"That's right," Darlene replied. "But I saw him more than our past employees. He wasn't…very good with people, I guess would be the best way to put it. He rubbed them the wrong way. I saw him a couple of times when Maria sent him home early, and I had to cover." She told herself to stop talking so much.

Officer Walsh wrote a couple of things down in the notebook, nodding. "Did you ever have a conversation with Jacob?"

Darlene tried to think. "Nothing important. Maybe just about the shop."

"Was he interested in the old books you sell here?"

"No. These are more for collectors and people interested in books that are in some strange subject areas."

He nodded. "Yes, I noticed you have a paranormal section. You must get some loonies interested in that area!" He laughed as if he told a funny joke.

Darlene bristled. She was one of the loonies he was making fun of. On top of that, he was wrong. At the very least, werewolves and vampires were real. She swallowed down any sarcastic remark she was going to make and forced a laugh.

"Yes," she replied. "What a lark." Darlene cringed to herself, thinking she sounded like she was eighty years old.

Officer Walsh didn't seem to notice that she was suddenly acting like an old lady and nodded in agreement with her. "Did Jacob ever mention leaving town or skipping out on anything?"

"No," Darlene replied, feeling useless with each question the cop asked.

"Did he have any debt that you were aware of?"

"No," she repeated, wondering why he was asking this when she had already made it clear that the two of them hadn't talked.

"Had he shown any interest in going into the bar down the street, *Roman's Tavern*?"

Darlene froze, taken aback for a moment. "*Roman's Tavern*?"

"Yeah, have you ever been there?" he responded. Darlene shook her head no, and Officer Walsh went on, "We have trouble there often. A lot of fighting and some pact there not to call the cops. Once in a while, some newbies will try to fit in there and are in over their heads. We spoke to someone who knew Jacob. Said he was thinking about going there."

Darlene shook her head, hoping she looked casual. "No. Sorry. No mention of *Roman's Tavern*. Not really my scene."

The cop nodded and stood up. "I think that'll be it."

Darlene stood up as well, and they walked out of Maria's office. Her mind was spinning. Why had Jacob been talking about going to *Roman's Tavern*? At first, Darlene thought that Jacob had merely run into Vivica somehow, and she had made a meal out of him. But now she was thinking that something far worse may have occurred. Officer Walsh said his good-byes.

Darlene wanted him to leave so she could text Idris. She wasn't in a hurry to see him on account of how she felt since they had slept together last night. She pushed the memories out of her head. This was more important than that.

Finally after Officer Walsh left the bookshop, Maria returned to her office looking pained. Darlene managed to send a text off to Idris that said only one thing: *We need to go to Roman's Tavern.*

Chapter Eight

Idris stared at the ceiling of his hotel room, all the while thinking of Darlene when his phone buzzed. A new text message arrived. He didn't move to get it right away. He couldn't get the thought of Darlene and last night out of his mind. When Idris had woken up and found that she had left already to go to work without leaving a note or saying anything to him, he wondered if they had made a mistake.

Darlene was clearly still upset and hurt over her last relationship. What if she only slept with him as a rebound? Did he sleep with her out of his own desire or did he have feelings for her as well? Maybe he had simply been too ramped up from the Change and wanted some physical release. He closed his eyes tightly, second guessing everything.

Now wasn't the time to get wrapped up in some human woman, he lectured himself. Lucian had something to do with Brent. He told Brent to try to get *The Book of the Ancients*. Why would he need such a thing?

Then something else came to him. It struck Idris so quickly that he didn't know why he hadn't thought of it sooner. Darlene said that Lucian had told her that someone would come looking for *The Werewolf Code*.

At the time, Idris thought the book was meant for him. What if it was for someone else? Whoever may have been working for Lucian was still going to come by for the book!

Idris sat up in bed and went to grab his phone. He had to text Darlene so she would know if anyone came by for that book to tell him right away. That was when he saw the text message from her. His heart thumped. He wasn't expecting any text from her. What was she going to say? Was she going to tell him they couldn't see each other anymore? Or that they made a mistake?

Idris opened the text message and read it.

We need to go to Roman's Tavern.

That was all it said. He was disappointed and relieved all at the same time. Darlene must have found something out, too. Idris stood up and grabbed his jacket. He headed out to the bookstore right away.

It took Idris only twenty minutes to make it to the shop. As he walked inside, he saw Darlene training the tiny old woman who had been recently hired. He felt his heart suddenly thump very hard in his chest. Idris tried to ignore it. Darlene looked up when he entered. She nodded at him before turning back to the woman… Mabel — that was the old woman's name. Idris wandered back to the supernatural section, looking for *The Werewolf Code*. He found it wedged between some book about ghosts and another about faeries.

Idris yanked it out and placed it on a table nearby. He didn't know what to look for, but there had to be a

reason that Lucian would take the book from the pack
and leave it here for someone to pick up. He idly
flipped through the pages he knew so well. Glancing
up, he made sure Mabel and Darlene were lost in
conversation as he slid out Brent's notebook with the
vampire paper scans in it. Why didn't Lucian have the
notebook already? That must mean that he didn't kill
Brent that night.

Idris glanced at what Brent had copied onto the thin
pages. The language was old and hard for Idris to even
understand. It looked like instructions on how to turn
someone into a vampire. Why did Lucian need this?
Why did he have Brent get these pages five years ago
and then leave this book here now?

Idris stopped suddenly at a page in the book. It was
near the start, explaining how to cause the Change in
someone. In the corner were Lucian's initials. This page
was meant for someone, too.

"What is he doing?"

Idris looked up to see Mabel looking at him. Her
skin was withered and old. Her hair was a mess of gray
tied up in a bun. Something about her unsettled him. It
was the way she looked at him. Suddenly Idris wanted
to get as far away from the old lady as possible. Had
she always been this unsettling? He hadn't paid
attention to her enough the first time Mabel showed up
for her interview.

"He's just looking at a book," Darlene replied, her
brow creasing in slight confusion over Mabel's sharp
tone.

Mabel's cloudy eyes lingered on Idris with a clarity he didn't like. No, there was something off about her, he decided. He just didn't know what it was. Her gaze fell to *The Werewolf Code*. Idris turned his back to her so he could look at the pages better and block her stares.

Darlene started speaking again, telling Mabel about the computer system. Idris studied the pages that Lucian had marked off. Both of the books had creation pages marked. Why? He felt as if he was banging his head against a wall. A few minutes later, Darlene ushered him over.

"I don't like your new hire," Idris mumbled to her.

"You think she was acting funny too?" Darlene whispered back.

Idris gave a slight nod and then briefly explained the connection he found with the books. In turn, Darlene explained to him how Jacob had mentioned going to *Roman's Tavern*.

"We should go, but I don't like leaving the store unattended. Someone is going to show up for this book. We could lay a trap for them. But I don't want you going to *Roman's Tavern* alone," Idris whispered.

Darlene chewed her bottom lip in thought. "I might be able to get a friend who can stay here and text us if anyone shows up."

"Contact your friend. We'll go to *Roman's Tavern* tonight then."

Darlene opened her mouth to speak when her phone went off. Darlene pulled it out and looked at it. Her face visibly paled. Idris felt his stomach drop even though he didn't know what happened yet.

"What?" Idris asked, harsher than he had meant to.

"I…" She faltered and tried again. "I set up a search alert for anything to do with Brent."

"And?"

Darlene glanced up at him. "Brent's mother was killed."

Darlene had to wait until break rolled around for her to contact Rebecca about coming down to watch the shop after closing. She felt odd calling her, knowing Rebecca would want to know why Darlene was making such a strange request. She was trying to come up with the most believable story that she could muster. But Darlene still felt distracted.

The news of Brent's mother's death cast an even darker cloud over her mood. There weren't many details on how she was murdered, but police disclosed that it was a break-in gone wrong. Darlene didn't believe that for a moment. Someone murdered Ms. Boots after they talked to her. Guilt wracked her. It was her idea to speak to Ms. Boots about Brent and now she was dead. Darlene felt another headache coming on.

That, plus Idris' sudden strange feeling about Mabel added to the issues. She found it strange how Mabel focused on Idris when he looked at *The Werewolf Code*. She tried to remember what she knew about Mabel but found mostly hazy memories. Darlene had been too busy with other things to pay attention to some old lady who wanted to work at a book store. She remembered mostly that she came in with an umbrella. The rest of the time with her seemed like a blur. She would have to pay better attention from now on.

Trying to shove the rest of her concerns from her mind, including being so close to Idris earlier that she wanted to touch him again, Darlene pulled out her phone. She unlocked the screen and stared at the article about Ms. Boots that she left up. Darlene shook her head as if to clear her thoughts and called Rebecca.

It rang for a little bit until she answered. "Darlene?" Her tone sounded surprised.

"Hey, Rebecca," Darlene breathed. "How are you?"

"I'm fine," Rebecca said, sounding a bit cautious. "What's up?"

"I was wondering if you can do me an odd favor."

Darlene then launched into her story.

It was 9:30 at night when Darlene's friend, Rebecca, pulled up into the parking lot behind the bookshop. Idris had a bad feeling in his gut about the entire thing. Darlene said that Rebecca was up for anything and liked adventure. That was fine, but this wasn't an adventure. Idris wasn't sure who was going to turn up to claim the book. He couldn't get Mabel's eyes out of his head. *She's an old lady… there is no way she can do anything.* He watched Rebecca get out of the car. She had short hair and big glasses and looked as if she weighed ten pounds. She was wearing all black and looked like a walking stereotype of what an artist in France would look like.

She waved and walked over to them, her boots clacking on the pavement. Earlier, Idris asked Darlene what she told her friend. Darlene told Rebecca that someone was going to break into the bookshop but they couldn't let anyone know. She told Rebecca it was highly dangerous and to lay low and text if anyone broke in and to not engage with them. Rebecca would have to park across the street in the front where she can observe the shop from the safety of her car. Rebecca jumped at the chance without hesitation. Idris hated the plan. But he told himself there was no promise of anyone actually breaking in for the book tonight. The only reason it felt like it might end up being tonight was because of Mabel, Ms. Boots' death and Jacob's disappearance. Everything seemed to roll at a high speed toward something terrible.

"Hey!" Rebecca said, cheerfully, pulling Darlene in for a hug. "Takes forever to see you and once I do, it's for something weird like this." Her brown-eyed gaze settled on Idris, clearly amused. "You must be Darlene's…friend." The way she paused on the word made Idris feel like anything but.

He shook her hand. "Nice to meet you."

"Same. So, you guys just want me to sit and watch the shop till you get back?" This was directed at Darlene, who nodded.

"If anyone or anything goes through that door, text me, okay? Rebecca, I'm going to stress this again — whoever goes through that door is going to be highly dangerous. We can't go to the police. You have to make sure they don't see you." She was chewing on her bottom lip, and Idris knew Darlene felt incredibly nervous as well.

Rebecca nodded. "I get it. I'm just keeping watch from the car while you guys do whatever other mystery thing you're doing."

"You don't mind doing this?" Idris spoke up.

Rebecca looked at him. "No. I mean, I'm not dumb. I'm sure there is way more going on than whatever Darlene told me." In the darkness, Idris could see Darlene flush. "But whatever it is, she is including me. More than we've hung out together lately, anyway. Besides, I'm all for adventure."

Idris still felt uneasy. Adventure, sure. But throwing this girl possibly in the way of Vivica or someone else made him worried.

"Okay," Darlene said. "We're going to go then, okay? Be careful."

They hugged again, and Idris and Darlene headed over to his pickup truck. Rebecca headed over to her car to move it up across the street in front of the shop.

"This is a bad idea," Darlene mumbled, looking up at the moon.

Idris' looked up at it as well. "Why? The full moon isn't for another week." That reminded him that he would have to hide from Darlene — there was no stopping the Change on a full moon.

She shook her head. "No. About Rebecca. I feel guilty. And after Ms. Boots…" Darlene trailed off.

Idris paused and then rested his hand on hers. "You told her it was extremely dangerous. You made it as clear as you could without saying it had to do with the supernatural."

Darlene looked at him and then nodded. "Let's go to *Roman's Tavern*."

Now it was his turn to feel nervous.

It didn't take long at all to get there. Darlene scrunched up the edges of her skirt in her hands. She was wrinkling it but didn't care. Her brain felt as if someone had taken it, put it in a blender and then poured it into a cup. She worried about Rebecca. Darlene wished she had told her about the vampires and werewolves instead of just stressing how dangerous it was. She had known Rebecca for a while. She was a daredevil and loved doing crazy things and calling it art. Of course, as soon as Darlene tried to warn her how dangerous it was, Rebecca leapt at the chance. On top of that, the guilt over Ms. Boots seemed to be a living creature inside of her. Darlene felt as if she had killed her herself. And then on top of that was this knowing feeling about Mabel. Was Idris just being crazy about her? Darlene had to stop thinking about it.

They pulled up in front of *Roman's Tavern*. It was crowded, with motorcycles and old trucks parked out front. She suddenly felt even more nervous.

Idris said, "They won't like outsiders. You're with me, and that will help a bit, but no one will be friendly to you."

Darlene steeled herself and nodded, opening the truck door. It was chilly, too cold for a skirt, but she barely felt the cold due to her nerves. How had Ms. Boots died? Was it Vivica? Did Vivica kill Jacob too? Darlene found herself looking at the rooftops of the buildings, just in case she was lying in wait. But there was nothing that popped out at her.

"Ready?" Idris asked.

Darlene stepped up next to him, feeling anything but ready.

They walked up to the doors, and Idris pulled one of them open. They were large and wooden, splintered in spots. They stepped inside, and Darlene tried to take everything in at once. There was a rock band off to the right side, playing loud music with a lead singer that howled into the mic, the tendons in his neck tight from screaming out words Darlene couldn't understand. A group of people were dancing, for lack of a better word, in front of the band. It mostly looked like thrashing.

The entire place stunk of cigarettes and old booze. There was a bar that wrapped around the other side with tables that looked as if they would crack if anyone sat at them. Most people stood.

There was a second floor above them, which was too dark to see anything. People probably went up there to do drugs and make out. As Idris had warned her, people were glaring at her. She felt exposed. Were all these people werewolves? How large was Roman's pack? Did Lucian's pack come here, too? She couldn't ask Idris anything because the terrible music was so loud. How was she going to ask anyone if they had seen Jacob?

Darlene felt Idris' strong fingers slide through hers and a shot of warmth went through her. She closed her eyes briefly as Idris pulled her through the crowd toward the bar. Idris stopped suddenly, and Darlene walked into his back, letting out a grunt of surprise. She peered around him to see another man talking to Idris. The man had a missing eye and was gesturing at her. Idris yelled something back but it was hard to hear.

"…humans….mental?" the one-eyed man yelled, pointing to Darlene.

Idris shouted back, "Looking…missing boy!"

The man shook his head in disgust at Idris. Darlene could tell they had some sort of history together. *He must be part of Roman's pack.* Idris said they were part of Roman's pack up until Brent turned up dead.

"Roman!" the one-eyed werewolf yelled and pointed to one corner.

Idris said something back and then tugged on Darlene, leading her through the crowd. Everywhere she looked, people glared at her, mostly in disgust. She felt more aware of her size than ever. No one else was as large as her. She wanted to leave. Why did she ever want to go to this bar?

There was a rundown table in this corner. A man who looked like he had giants as parents sat there along with a trashy-looking woman with a shaved head that made her look sickly and a dress that probably cost twenty dollars around forty years ago. She glared at Darlene as well. Darlene averted her gaze. The man stood up and Darlene was struck by how large he was. He could probably kill anything that came toward him. *He must be the pack leader.*

"What are you doing, Idris?" the man grunted, getting very close to Idris. "Have you lost your mind?"

"I'm looking for the boy who just went missing, Roman."

"Not my concern if another human went missing. And who the hell is this?" Roman jutted his chin toward Darlene, who tried to look brave.

"Friend of the missing boy."

Roman sneered, "That all, Idris? She looks to be about the size you like."

Darlene felt her entire face flush red. *Asshole,* she thought, wanting to tell him off but not feeling like getting killed. The woman behind Roman let out a laugh. Idris growled and jerked forward, his face now inches from Roman. Darlene could only watch.

Roman was looking at Idris now. "You find your missing pack leader yet? You know, I've been hearing some funny things about your best friend lately. Heard he was fucking your old vamp girl. What was her name? Vivica?"

Darlene had never seen Idris so angry. She balked, wishing she could be anywhere else.

"Have you seen the boy?" Idris repeated.

Roman stared at him. "I didn't see him. You probably killed him though… just like you killed that kid five years ago."

That was enough for Idris to snap. Darlene thought it could have been the stress of everything that finally got to him. She wasn't sure. All she saw was Idris leap and knock Roman down to the ground. The two of them smashed against the table. Darlene jumped back and could only watch in horror as Idris slammed his fist directly into Roman's face. The woman at the table jumped and flew toward Idris. Idris shoved her away and two other people held the woman back.

Roman swung his fist toward Idris, connecting with his lower jaw. There was a disgusting noise. The music was still playing. Some people didn't even look over. This must be an every night thing. She wasn't sure what to do. How does one stop werewolves from killing each other? Idris picked Roman up by the collar of his shirt and slammed him against the wall before head butting him. Roman's nose began to bleed and Darlene felt pretty confident that it was broken. No one was going to break up the fight, she realized with a sinking feeling.

She turned around to see if anyone else was going to do anything about it, but no one moved. The group nearby watched as casually as if they were watching TV. Darlene was just about to turn back around when she saw something that made her stop. Someone walked behind the bar… the curve of the neck and that shaggy hair. The person turned slightly to the left, and Darlene's heart thumped a bit harder.

Jacob.

Darlene snapped her head back to see Idris and Roman still fighting. Suddenly irritated at both Idris and the other pack leader, she stormed over to them. She yanked back on Idris' shirt. Normally that wouldn't have done anything, but he was taken aback and lost his footing, his knees hitting the ground. Roman was slumped against the wall, his face covered in blood and his breathing ragged.

"Can you get a grip? Both of you?" she snapped, louder than she had meant to because some people were looking at her curiously now.

Idris looked abashed. "Darlene…"

She yanked him up as he stumbled to his feet and hissed in his ear, "Jacob is here."

His eyes widened in surprise. Darlene looked at Roman one last time as the woman ran over and crouched next to him, glaring at Idris. Darlene turned around and made her way through the crowd.

"…Broke up the fight…"

"…Human getting involved…"

"Kinda cute for a big girl," said one guy as Darlene walked by.

Irritated, she flipped the man off as she picked up her pace, walking behind the bar. There were protests from the bartender but Idris said something that shut him up quickly. Darlene's heart thumped some more. Jacob was alive and here in this bar. Idris and Darlene burst through the back exit behind the bar, the music spilling out behind them. No one was there.

"I am sure he came this way," she said to Idris.

"You're positive it was him?" Idris said, trying to rub Roman's blood out of his shirt.

She nodded. "I swear it was him." She looked at Idris. "What was that about?"

"What?" Idris replied, clearly playing dumb. When Darlene didn't say anything back, Idris looked sheepish. "He pisses me off."

"Is that how werewolves settle disagreements?"

"Pretty much."

Darlene thought about making another quip when she saw a shadow move behind Idris. Without thinking, she took off toward it, pushing Idris out of the way. Idris chased after it as well. She could see the outline of Jacob's face in the darkness. He was against a brick wall that blocked the alleyway next to the bar. In the dim moonlight, Darlene made out the whites of his eyes.

And then suddenly, Jacob leapt up in the air and over the wall. It was graceful and fluid, like a bird. In a single motion, he was gone. Darlene stopped running and stared at the top of the wall. Her throat had gone dry. She knew that motion. Jacob was a vampire.

Just then her phone chirped in her purse. With a sinking feeling in her stomach, Darlene yanked it out. She got the text ten minutes ago but didn't hear it during the commotion in the bar. With shaking fingers Darlene opened up the text. It said one word.

Help.

Chapter Nine

They sped down the road toward the bookshop as quickly as they could. Luckily they weren't far and got there in a couple of minutes. Idris' heart was beating fast. He glanced over at Darlene, who looked as pale as a ghost. He cursed himself for wasting time fighting with Roman like that. Roman urged him to fight, made remarks to get under his skin, and Idris took the bait. He should have just walked away.

Instead he had quickly and easily fallen back into his old behavior. The same behavior he told himself and Lucian he would no longer do. He scowled at the thought of Lucian. So much for being on the straight and narrow, when Lucian was plotting and planning something for years behind his back.

And now Jacob was a vampire. Why did Vivica bother to turn that boy into one? And Roman…did he mean it when he said Lucian and Vivica had a thing going on?

"Stop!" Darlene cried.

Idris slammed on the breaks. He almost drove right by the bookstore, too involved with his own thoughts yet again. On the street, Rebecca's car sat where they last saw it parked but there was no Rebecca. The door to the bookshop was flung wide open, with light spilling out onto the sidewalk. Darlene flew out of the car. Idris cursed and took off after her, trying to stay by Darlene's side.

They ran into the bookshop. Books were strewn around the room, some with the covers torn off. The computer had been flung off the desk and was shattered. Some of the shelves were tipped over and the lights were flashing. Bulbs were popped, Idris realized as he tried to get used to the flickering lights. He ground his teeth, fighting off the urge to Change.

"Rebecca!" Darlene called. "Rebecca!"

"I took care of your friend," said a voice — one that Idris knew very well.

Vivica came around one of the bookshelves. Her red hair was loose and flowing over her shoulders. She wore all black. Her red eyes were dark and stormy. She would have been beautiful, if it hadn't been for the blood smeared around her mouth.

"No!" Darlene cried when she saw Vivica's mouth, lurching forward.

Idris pulled her back and behind him, putting himself between the two of them.

Vivica scowled. "Protecting her? Won't do you any good. Where is it?"

"Where is what, Vivica?" Idris replied, sounding like a tired father dealing with a spoiled kid.

Her eyes narrowed. "You had that girl protecting *The Werewolf Code*. I have that now. *The Book of the Ancients* — I need it. Where is it?"

"You're a vampire. You don't have a copy of it?"

"No," Vivica spat. "Our copy doesn't have what I need. And Lucian told me he'd have *The Werewolf Code* here plus *The Book of the Ancients*. So where is it?"

Darlene spoke up, "We never had that book."

Worry creased Vivica's face. "The pages then, the pages that stupid boy did five years ago. Give me those. I know you have them. I went to his mother's last night to find them. Lucian said Brent had them. And since I couldn't find our book, the copies he made would have to do."

"You killed Brent's mother?"

"I was hungry," Vivica replied coldly.

Idris tried to sort out what she said while stalling until he could figure out a way to take her down. "You're working with Lucian?"

Vivica began to pace the room now, her long legs making her look almost like a cat. "Lucian and I have been working together for years. You were just too stupid to see it, Idris. You believed anything I told you in our disgusting relationship." She shrugged. "But Lucian didn't want to do anything physical with me. Said it took things too far. So I had my fun… with you. Lucian had *The Werewolf Code*. But he needed *The*

Book of the Ancients for his plan. Brent was the perfect patsy and so willing to get the pages."

"Why couldn't you get the pages?" Idris said as Darlene whimpered, still not seeing Rebecca. "It is your book, after all."

"Lucian didn't want our copy. Said it was missing too much. He knew of a copy that was directly from the original, from a rival clan. I couldn't go in and get it. We got Brent to do it. Lucian told him he'd make him a werewolf if he did. Brent made copies of the pages we needed. All the information about turning, including the information that had been lost to the ages."

"That was five years ago," Idris countered, trying to cover Darlene as she moved closer to the ground, getting ready to crawl under an overturned table to get out of Vivica's line of vision. "Did you kill Brent and then decide against whatever ridiculous plan you had going?"

Vivica snorted, still pacing. "No. We didn't kill Brent. I don't know who did. That was when Roman told Lucian he had to go. Roman backed out of the plan then. Said the heat coming down on him was too heavy now that Brent showed up dead. He tried to pin it on you, but you didn't buy it. So Lucian split from the pack."

"Roman was in on the plan?" Idris repeated.

Vivica scowled. "That's right, pup. Lucian decided to lay low. Make Roman think he had given up on his plan. Buy Roman's trust with time."

Idris didn't know where Darlene was. He hoped she had somehow gotten around Vivica to Maria's office. Rebecca could be in there. Vivica was too involved in her own speech to notice Darlene had gone missing. She always did love to talk. Idris decided to keep her talking.

"So he stopped whatever he was doing for five years?"

"Yes. But he's been trying again. We need those pages though, from the book of our kind. You have to have them. I know you were snooping around for Lucian. I have that old human spy for me. Mabel. She's loyal to me. Thinks I'll make her a vampire before the cancer eats away at her. I won't. You know that. But she told me you were snooping around here for that book. I thought she meant the vampire one until tonight when she told me you were looking at *The Werewolf Code*."

"Lucian said he left it here for someone."

"He left it here for me."

"Where is he?"

"He's in hiding. He wants me to get the vampire pages we need and *The Werewolf Code* and then he'll contact me and let me know where he is."

"Why is he in hiding?"

Vivica groaned. "You ask so many questions about things I can't tell you, Idris. The only reason I've told you this much already is because I thought you would want to know before I kill you right here, right now."

She bared her fangs and, in a flash, Vivica slammed into him. Idris went flying back, smashing against a bookshelf. He tried to clear the fog that settled around his head. Memories flashed by, now coupled with the truth. Lucian had used Brent to get the vampire pages. Someone had killed Brent. Roman knew Lucian's plan. Vivica had been with Lucian, who'd left *The Werewolf Code* for a vampire minion to pick up.

Whatever grand scheme Lucian had going, it wouldn't be enough to right the wrongs he had already created. Rage burned hot in Idris. Vivica stared at him, her pretty features twisted in a sneer.

"You going to Change on me, pup?"

Idris started to see red. *Yes, I am going to Change.*

But this time he welcomed it.

Darlene managed to crawl toward Maria's office without Vivica seeing her. She loved to talk. Darlene could tell by the tone of her voice that she relished every moment she crushed Idris over the memory of Lucian. As Darlene crawled behind the desk, she could see the door to Maria's office was nudged open a crack. Rebecca had to be in there. Darlene's heart pounded loudly in her ears. She was amazed no one else could hear it.

She crawled over to the door and slid it open painfully slowly. She hoped Vivica wouldn't notice. She needed Vivica not to notice so she could get inside.

From what Darlene could gather, Lucian was working with Vivica. Why did he leave the book here, of all places? Why couldn't he just meet up with Vivica and give her the book? Did he just want Mabel to steal the book and give it to Vivica? Darlene felt as if Vivica was being lied to in some regard about why Lucian left the werewolf book here, but she couldn't figure it out. Not now. Not when she slowly slid the door open and saw a pale hand jutting out from behind the couch.

Darlene crawled over as quickly as she could. The entire office was trashed. Maria's desk was cracked in two with papers all over the floor. The chair that Officer Walsh sat on only hours ago had been smashed against the wall. The couch was sitting on the floor, lop-sided. Darlene held her breath and looked behind it.

Rebecca was on her back. Her eyes were closed. Her skin was deathly pale. Her neck was covered in blood. Her glasses were smashed and lying by her side. Fear, cold and clammy, came alive in Darlene's stomach. She was going to throw up.

Outside the office, she heard a smash and then books falling. She closed her eyes briefly. Idris would have to handle Vivica. Rebecca was wounded because Darlene had thrown her into this mess. Darlene went over to her and felt for a pulse. She couldn't feel one, but she wasn't sure if that was because of her own fear clouding her brain. She fumbled for her phone to call an ambulance. Darlene tilted Rebecca's head to one side and her heart stopped.

Rebecca's neck had two little puncture marks.

"It's been a while since I've seen you Change, Idris. You know, since you were trying to be a good little dog."

Idris snarled at her. Vampires didn't have any scent. He wasn't sure what bookshelf she hid behind now. Every muscle in his body felt alive. With Idris in his werewolf form, the only thing he cared about was attacking and defending accordingly. Everything else faded. That was why he used to love the Change. He never had to think when he was in his werewolf form.

"I wonder if your new girlfriend found her friend yet. I was thinking about just killing her, you know? But I decided against it."

Idris growled, pacing the floor, trying to find her. There was a flash of red, and she appeared next to him. He pushed off the floor with his hind legs and smashed into her. The two of them went flying into a table, which smashed in half underneath them. Idris bit down on her shoulder and sunk his teeth in. It was like biting stone. Vampire skin was just layers of dead skin being held alive by some disgusting force. Vivica thrashed underneath him and kicked him in his stomach. Idris let out a whine and was suddenly thrust into the air before hitting the ground.

"I thought to myself, would Lucian kill her? No, he wouldn't. He needs loyal servants to come to him later, once he has figured it out completely."

Idris leapt to his feet again and ran forward, ready to clamp down on Vivica's face and destroy her. He was sick of hearing her speak. He bit down on her ankle and tugged. Surprised, she toppled to the ground. Idris raised his front paws and extended his claws, bringing them down on her back, hard.

Vivica let out a gasp. Idris wasn't sure how much pain he caused her. There were only a few ways to kill vampires and, sadly, clawing them in the back wasn't one of them. Idris didn't feel the usual satisfaction he got when he fought with someone, because he was fighting a vampire and no one actually alive.

Vivica rolled over and grabbed Idris' neck. She tossed him off, and he skidded across the floor. That was another thing he hated. Vampire strength made him feel like a rag doll being tossed around.

Vivica looked at him, her red eyes flashing with pleasure. "I turned her, Idris. I turned your new girlfriend's friend into one of us. And when Lucian figures out how to combine both vampire and werewolves into one species, she'll be the first in line for the fucking experiment."

<<◇>>

Darlene spoke rapidly into her phone, "No, I need an ambulance here right away! There's been a break in, and my friend has been attacked!"

Rebecca still wasn't moving. Her chest had stopped slowly rising up and down. Fear clutched at Darlene. *No, no, this can't be happening. Not to Rebecca.* The operator said they were dispatching someone right away, and Darlene hung up.

"Rebecca," she whispered to her friend. "Please wake up."

She shouldn't have asked Rebecca for her help. Why in the world did she leave the safety of her car? What a mistake it was. Panic, rage and sadness boiled up inside of her. Tears sprang from the corners of her eyes. She killed her friend.

Rebecca's eyes suddenly opened. And they were red.

Idris threw himself at Vivica again, and they toppled into the wall. Vivica looked irritated, which was the best Idris could say he was doing. He hated to admit it, but he was outmatched. Vivica was an ancient vampire. On top of that, they had been together on and off for a long time and often would fight with one another. They knew each other's weaknesses.

Combining werewolves and vampires. What sort of fucked up idea was that? How could Lucian be plotting such a thing? He cast a glance over to Maria's office. Darlene was in there. Was she safe if Rebecca truly turned?

Vivica loomed over him, ready to strike again. One of his paws bled from when she sank her fangs into him moments before. She tasted blood and wanted more. But suddenly a siren filled the air. Vivica's head snapped up, and she looked back at him.

"Your bitch must have called the cops," she hissed through her fangs. "Tell her I'll be back for my new baby."

And Vivica was gone, bursting through the nearest window into the night, scaling the walls of the coffee shop next door. The sirens grew louder. He needed to Change back and it had to be now. But it was hard to come down from the negative emotions he felt. He wouldn't be able to Change back in time.

Darlene let out a gasp of surprise and lurched backward. Rebecca sat up so quickly that it looked almost like a blur. Rebecca stared at her now, wide-eyed and panicked. She grabbed her neck, feeling it, making soft noises that Darlene couldn't make out. Rebecca suddenly let out a cry of sharp pain and looked down at her hand. She had accidently touched her cross necklace. Darlene could see the faint burn mark on her neckline as well as her hand.

Sirens. The ambulance was coming, but Darlene now regretted calling them. Rebecca heard them, too. With a scream, she wrapped her hand around the necklace and ripped it off of her neck, tossing it onto the floor.

"Rebecca," Darlene whispered.

Her eyes focused on Darlene for a moment. She looked terrifying, with her pale, dead-looking skin and blood smeared along her neck and T-shirt. And the bite marks. Those bite marks.

Rebecca let out another scream, and Darlene saw the fangs in her mouth. Then, in a flash, she ran past Darlene and burst out of the office. Darlene stumbled to her feet. She felt as if her head had been held underwater for too long. Her movements felt sluggish and slow compared to Rebecca's. She opened the door to Maria's office as the paramedics and cops burst in.

She was the only one left in the book store. Even Idris was gone.

Chapter Ten

Hazy. That was the only word Darlene could use to describe the next few hours. The police asked tons of questions that she stumbled through. She stammered out that her friend had gotten up and left. No, she didn't know where she had gone. No, she didn't know who had broken in or where they had gone. Yes, she was fine, she just had a headache.

It wasn't until Officer Walsh came into the room and gave her a cup of coffee that she became dimly aware of her surroundings. He sat across from her, and Darlene watched his mouth move but she didn't hear anything.

Rebecca. That was her only thought since she saw Rebecca's red eyes. Vivica turned her only friend into a vampire. And it was all her fault. She turned Rebecca herself by asking her to watch the shop... just like she had killed Ms. Boots.

"Miss Troop?" The sound of her last name jolted her back to the present day.

Darlene shook her head and tried to focus on Officer Walsh. "I'm sorry. What did you say?"

"I said that I had looked into your story a bit after your call came in. You were here at the station a few days ago, claiming you had information on Brent Boots."

That felt like a lifetime ago. Was it truly only a few days ago? In any case, she nodded.

"A neighbor of Ms. Boots said she saw someone fitting your description and another man visiting her the day of her murder."

Yes, it's my fault. All of it was my fault. If I had only minded my own business when Idris showed up. If I had only remained a hermit. None of this would have happened to anyone.

But instead she just nodded again.

"Miss Troop, I understand you're in shock from whatever happened at the book store. But I need to know why you saw Ms. Boots on the day of her murder."

Darlene opened her mouth to reply when suddenly the door to the room opened. Another officer peeked inside with a strained expression on his face.

"What?" barked Officer Walsh.

The man's eyes darted to Darlene. "There's a man here for Miss Troop. He won't leave. Demanded to see her now."

Idris. Darlene stood up quickly and, without saying anything else to Officer Walsh, pushed past the man at the door and walked down the hall quickly. Her heart thrummed with his name. She needed to see him. She needed to know that Idris, at the very least, was okay.

She burst through the door of the hallway and out into the main station floor. Her eyes scanned the area. Maria sat in one corner, talking to an officer with panic spread all across her face. Darlene half expected to see Vivica there, her hands held together by handcuffs, with her leg casually thrown over one side of a chair, staring at her. Then she saw him.

Idris stood in front of the main desk. His face looked drawn and his eyes tired, as if he hadn't slept in ages. His clothes were baggy, hanging off of him in odd angles, as if they weren't even his. Idris' eyes darted around, searching for Darlene. She moved forward now, toward the exhausted werewolf she suddenly wanted more than anything.

Idris finally saw Darlene. She moved toward him, as if she was a ghost. Her skin was deathly pale, almost as if she was a vampire herself. Her hair stuck up at odd angles, and her eyes had purple circles under them. Her clothes were wrinkled and her blue eyes seemed to have a funny look to them. His heart pounded as she walked over to him.

When Idris realized there was no way to Change back in time before the ambulance and police arrived, he fled. He hated himself every second he spent turning around and running out through the back door. He scrambled into the parking lot and jumped the brick wall, crashing into the bushes beyond. But even that wasn't good enough, because the police were soon checking the area, trying to find whoever Darlene had told them had broken into the store. Idris, still in his werewolf form, fled even farther away from Darlene. He ran into the woods to where Brent had been found murdered.

The emotions inside him were too strong to Change back. He never had this problem before. Normally, the rage in him would quell after a battle. The only time he couldn't Change back was during a full moon.

But now it was too much. There was no stopping the onslaught of feelings inside of him. *Combine both werewolves and vampires into one species.* The words kept repeating in his skull, bouncing around as if his brain had been turned into a dozen beach balls. How could Lucian be plotting such a reckless act? And why?

He reviewed everything Vivica said a million times over. Lucian got Brent involved to get the pages from the vampire book. He dropped the idea once Brent was discovered murdered by someone and didn't have the pages. He was trying the stupid idea all over again.

Something nagged at him though. Idris understood not having the vampire pages detailing the art of turning a victim. But Lucian *had* the book of the werewolves, explaining everything about how to turn someone into a werewolf. Why would he drop it off at the bookstore for someone to pick up, only to collect it for him again? It seemed redundant. Vivica claiming it had been for her and her spy, Mabel, seemed wrong. As if Vivica had been lied to.

Vivica killed Ms. Boots. But she didn't mention changing Jacob. Was there a link between Jacob working at the store and now being a vampire? Vivica rarely changed people into vampires. She hated taking care of the younglings. Idris knew she had changed Darlene's friend out of spite and was going to leave her out to dry until she could experiment on her.

That meant there was a feral vampire out there somewhere.

It took Idris four hours to Change back. Once he did, he headed to the police station right away after Darlene didn't pick up her phone.

And now she was standing in front of him, her eyes no longer that bright blue he adored but a somber dark hue that showed nothing but pain. Idris let out a grunt and pulled her close to him, engulfing her in his arms, clutching her close. Her hands wrapped around his, and they stood there like that, in the midst of the police station and the buzz of activity, for quite some time.

By the time the police finally released Darlene, she felt exhausted and dirty. She craved a shower and sleep. Officer Walsh was furious that she left before her questioning was finished, but Idris had pulled himself up to full size and stared at him until he relented. But Darlene knew he'd be back with more questions. She had no problem explaining the things she had found about Brent online, but it was harder to come up with a convincing story about why she had gone to see Ms. Boots, who then wound up dead.

Darlene lied and said Rebecca came into town and wanted to pop in for a book before they met up. Then Darlene got the text, ran to the book store and found Rebecca wounded. She called 911 before the assailant attacked her, knocking her out. When Darlene came to, Rebecca was gone and the cops had just arrived.

Darlene knew that if the cops really started looking into the story, they would find pieces that didn't make any sense. Like the fact that Darlene had been at *Roman's Tavern* moments before when Idris had gotten into that fight. It wasn't as if they had lain low when they were there. Then Officer Walsh would come back with more questions that Darlene wasn't sure how to explain. He'd want to talk to Idris, too. Cops were going out to search for Rebecca.

Darlene didn't know much about young vampires. She barely knew anything about vampires in general, having not known they were real until recently. She found herself missing the days when she would read the supernatural books in the shop and knew it was all made up.

She thought back to the night in her apartment complex parking lot, when Vivica and Idris fought. The transparent shape in the woods nearby. The thought would come back to her once in a while, almost as if it was trying to tell her something.

"Darlene."

She shook her head and looked up to see they were at her apartment complex. She found herself gazing at the woods. But in the morning sunlight, there was nothing out of the ordinary to be seen.

"Let me walk you inside."

Darlene nodded and they got out of the truck. She suddenly wanted Idris. What did it say about her — about the fact that she wanted to sleep with him again just so she could stop thinking and feel as if someone truly cared about her? It probably said a lot, none of which actually interested her at the moment.

As she walked into her apartment and Idris stepped in behind her, Darlene turned around and kissed him. Idris let out a noise of surprise as she pushed herself against him, the door shutting behind him as she pulled at his clothes. Idris responded by kissing along her neck, mumbling her name. He smelled like the woods, Darlene noticed, as she tugged his shirt off. Her hands trailed over his muscles again, liking the feel of them under her fingers.

"You're so beautiful," Idris groaned in her ear as they toppled onto her couch.

This time their kisses were different. They were hard, fast and filled with a sense of growing dread, as if the entire world was going to change right before them and all they had was this moment. Darlene was Idris' rock, and he was hers. Gone were thoughts of the bookstore, Vivica's red eyes and Rebecca fleeing. Gone were images of Officer Walsh and Ms. Boots. All Darlene had was Idris undressing in front of her, enflaming her with desire.

She lay on the couch, looking up at him as he took off his clothes. Soon Idris only had his boxers on. Darlene saw his hard shaft straining against the fabric. She tugged them down and ran her tongue along his length. Idris shuddered as Darlene slowly, agonizingly, ran her tongue along him. Up and down, up and down. She looked up at him and when their gazes met, Idris let out a soft moan. Darlene liked being in control. She slid the head of his shaft into her mouth and sucked gently. Idris grunted in response as she then slid him out of her mouth again, teasing him.

"Darlene…" he groaned.

She liked how hard he was and how warm he was. He was even warmer than usual, if that was possible. Darlene took him back into her mouth, this time as far as she could take him. Idris moaned and arched his hips, forcing more of him in. Darlene let him fill up her mouth and throat, her eyes closing in delight. She loved how well he fit. Her underwear clung to her wetness as she worked him again. She moved her head up and down on him until Idris suddenly lurched away. She looked up at him in surprise.

"No more. Let me have you."

Darlene nodded and turned around on the couch, wanting him to take her from behind. Idris didn't even bother pulling down her underwear. He ripped them off of her. He pushed up her skirt and slid inside her. Darlene was so wet that she accepted him instantly. She moaned, the full length of him filling her up. Idris felt so amazing. He began to pump in her, hard and fast.

She loved the feel of him. She loved that she could make him feel this good and how he wanted her this much.

Darlene moved against him, taking him all. His hands tangled up in her hair, and he pulled on it when he thrust into her. Darlene arched her back, her clothes stuck to her, throwing her head back, letting out a moan. Sucking him had made her so turned on that she was ready to come. Idris slammed into her, his breathing hard and heavy.

"Idris!"

Darlene shuddered, shutting her eyes tightly as her orgasm shook her. The pleasure vibrated through her body. At the same time, Idris yelled her name, louder than ever, loud enough that she was sure the neighbors could hear it. He slammed into her again, and she felt him coming, filling her up. This heightened her orgasm more. Darlene rocked her hips, milking him, moaning loudly, overcome by the pleasure of it all. Her mind was blank and empty. All she cared about was her orgasm.

Idris grunted too as he came, mumbling her name like a chant as he finished. Darlene slumped against the couch, panting for breath. He slid out of her and slumped to the floor, his chest heaving. Darlene rolled off the couch and moved toward him.

There, on the floor of her living room, the two of them fell asleep, entwined and naked.

Chapter Eleven

Idris knew this was a bad idea. But there was no way he wasn't going to see Roman that afternoon. If he ended up in another fight, then so be it.

He had woken up in Darlene's arms an hour ago. She was still sleeping soundly. Idris draped a blanket over her and left a note, explaining what he was going to do. He didn't like leaving her there. Was he falling for Darlene because she knew who he was and didn't leave him? Or was he falling for her because their situation made it almost impossible not to?

And what if he was falling for her because of only positive reasons — what about Darlene? She still had that framed photo of her ex on her night table. Was she ready for another relationship?

Instead of lying there next to her over-thinking it, he decided to leave and find Roman. He had to find out what he knew about Lucian and Vivica and their plan.

Idris pushed open the doors of the bar and was greeted with the same sights as the last time. This time Roman was talking to Mark in the center of the floor with Julie next to him. She saw him first and glared. She was there at the fight last night and would have probably torn Idris to shreds if Roman had allowed it.

"What the hell are you doing here?" Julie stormed over to him, her eyes already dilating, trying to fight off the Change.

Idris ignored her. "Roman, I need to speak to you."

Mark stepped in front of him. "He doesn't want to speak to you."

"What, Roman can't make his own decisions on who to speak to? He has to have his lackeys do all the talking?"

Idris knew that would be enough to irritate Roman, and he was right. Roman shoved Mark aside and walked over to him. His nose was bandaged up from where Idris broke it and one side of his face had swollen up. Idris won that fight. He had only a few bruises and nothing broken. Roman must be pissed.

Roman stood at his full height and looked down at Idris. "You come to play nice, pup?"

"We need to talk. Actually talk."

"I'm busy."

"With what?"

"Idris?"

Idris turned around to see who had called his name. On the second floor was a tall, lean Asian woman with her hair swept up in a messy bun. She was wearing jeans and an oversized T-shirt. Her eyes were wide.

Idris hadn't seen her since her crying fit over Lucian.
Liara — Lucian's'wife.

"Liara! What are you doing here?"

Liara walked down the steps. Her high heels made
sharp noises against the stairs. She came over to him
and hugged him. She always smelled like flowers.

"I haven't heard from you in a while. And nothing
from Lucian either. Our pack is in trouble with both of
you missing. And…" She hesitated, glancing over at
Roman before lowering her voice. "Idris, our copy of
The Werewolf Code is missing."

They both knew what that meant. Without their
copy of the book, they were no longer a pack. Idris
knew he would have to give Liara the book and
discover who it was meant for later.

"Talk to me after this," Idris whispered before
turning back to Roman. "Can we speak alone?"

Roman paused and then nodded. He brushed Julie
off, who was telling him not to and walked up the stairs
toward his office.

Idris turned and stopped in front of Liara. "The
book is at a book store down the street. Leave, go right
and keep walking. Get the book."

Liara seemed shaken but nodded as Idris walked by
her. Whoever was meant to have the book would find
out and be pissed off, but as long as Liara had it, they
would still be a pack. If Liara claimed the book, she'd

be pack leader next. It might be better for everyone if she was.

Idris stepped inside Roman's office again as he sat down at his desk.

"Listen, I don't want to talk to you. But it wouldn't do for us to fight again. Julie would just get on my ass. So whatever you want to say, just say it and leave." He leaned back, grabbing a cigarette out of his pocket.

Idris remained standing. "Five years ago, Lucian worked with Vivica to cross our blood line and create some disgusting hybrid. You knew about this."

Roman went still. Surprise flickered across his face before he managed to put a bored expression on. "Figured you knew."

"You knew I had no idea. Who killed Brent?"

There was a long pause now as Roman lit up the cigarette and watched the tip burn. Idris felt hot all over and itchy, wanting to lunge and beat the answers out of Roman. *Deep breathing, stay focused.*

"I did."

"Why?"

"I thought if Brent was killed, Lucian would give up his ridiculous plan. I knew he was using the boy to try to get pages from that damned vampire book. He needed information on both werewolf transformation and the full details of vampire transformations, which not all the copies have. I thought if I killed Brent, he'd lose his little helper and give up the plan."

"It didn't work, did you know that? Lucian is trying it again. Did you kill Lucian?"

"No. No, I didn't kill Lucian, although I wish I had. I don't know where he is. And I don't care. If he's dead, that means that ridiculous plan of his is dead, too."

"He's not dead. He's working with Vivica."

"That crazy bitch," Roman mumbled, taking a drag off his cigarette. "Listen, pup, I'll tell you the only thing I know about Lucian's disappearance. He told me he wanted the pack to reform. He didn't want to be pack leader anymore, and he didn't trust you to do it. He told me he was going to give me *The Werewolf Code*. Said he'd leave it in town and tell me where to pick it up. Never heard from him since, and now he's vanished. So you have your pack, but barely." He leaned forward, staring at Idris. "But once I find that book, your pack is under my control again, understand? And we can move on from this nightmare Lucian tried to bring to light."

Idris felt relief wash over him that he told Liara to get the book from Darlene's shop. And then that sick sense of betrayal washed over him yet again. Lucian giving the pack to Roman…had he really thought Idris couldn't handle the pack on his own? *Maybe I can't, but Liara can.*

"Roman, I don't like you. But you know that. You don't like me either. So listen to me when I tell you that I don't think Lucian is dead. He's still working with Vivica. He sent her after me to try to get pages from the vampire book to learn more about the transformation. He may have promised you the pack, but he hasn't dropped his idea. He's just gone rogue."

"What do you want me to do? Not my concern."

"No, it is your fucking concern," Idris snapped, slamming his hands on Roman's desk. "You knew about this terrible idea and yet did nothing to stop it."

Roman growled, "I killed Brent! I tried to stop it. What the hell did you do, Idris? Fuck vampires and piss everyone off? You're still barely in control of yourself. Even now, what are you doing to stop it or are you fucking the bookstore girl, too?"

Rage filled Idris' veins as he tried to control his breathing before speaking again. "There's another thing to look out for. Vivica created a vampire and left her. The girl escaped. There's a feral vampire on the loose."

"Fantastic," Roman replied, his voice dry.

Idris stood back up, watching Roman smoke. "One more thing. Why was a vampire at your club last night?"

His gaze faltered for a moment. "What?"

"You heard me. You had a newborn vamp at your club last night. Darlene knows the kid. Around Brent's age. Why was he sneaking around here and not being attacked by your thug pack?"

"I don't know of any young vampire in my club." Roman spat on the floor and stood up, a growl coming from his throat. "I told you what I knew about Lucian. I told you I killed Brent. I told you I'm going to find out where Lucian put the book of our people and I'm going to dismantle your pack. I don't know shit about some kid vamp running around in my bar. But if I see him, I'll make sure I end him myself. Got it?"

Idris leaned close to him, inches from his face, close enough to smell the tobacco from Roman's breath. "If I find out you're lying to me about anything else, my next visit won't be so pretty." He took a step back. "You might want to put some ice on your nose."

Idris stormed out of the room, taking deep breaths, trying to control himself from Changing. As he turned the corner back out onto the second floor of the club, he ran into Julie. She thudded against him and bounced off before straightening up.

"Were you trying to eavesdrop on us?"

"No."

"You're lying."

Julie's small, thin frame was wrecked by hard drug usage over the years. Her eyes constantly looked on the verge of bugging out. Her tattoos were faded in spots and she was constantly dirty. She had missing teeth from poor dental care and constant fights with other females in the pack. Idris didn't know how she ever aligned herself with Roman but as far as he was concerned, they were a perfect match for each other.

But now as she stared at him, her usual hostility was gone. In its place was something weird — a look he had never seen before in her.

"What?" Idris snapped.

"That girlfriend of yours," Julie started, glancing over her shoulder. "You better be careful with her."

"Why?"

"She ain't like normal folk, Idris. I hope you weren't stupid enough to tell her what we is. Because it's going to come back on you, hard and fast. Especially if she ever realizes what she can do."

Idris' head thrummed with a dull pain, "What she can do? What are you talking about?"

"I warned you."

Julie slinked into the hallway and headed to Roman's office. Idris stood there for a moment, trying to make sense of what Julie had spouted before shaking his head and heading down the stairs.

Maria fiddled with the same book, opening and closing it, for over twenty minutes now, as she looked around the bookshop. Darlene never saw her so upset before. She cleaned up the store as Maria stood there, sending out wave after wave of confused, distracting energy. Darlene kept thinking about Rebecca — where was she right now? Then her mind would go to Jacob — who changed him and what was he doing? To Idris — should she keep sleeping with him? She liked him more than she wanted to admit, but was it only because of their circumstances? And now Maria was hovering, constantly looking at Darlene, clearly not believing her story at all.

Darlene was going to open her mouth and finally break the agonizing silence when the bell above the door rang out.

"We're closed," Maria said.

"Oh, I'm sorry…I was told to come here…"

Darlene turned around to see a tall, gorgeous Asian woman standing in the doorway. Her clothes were simple, but she radiated a sadness that almost knocked Darlene over.

"How can I help you?" she asked the woman.

"Idris sent me. He said you had a book here called *The Werewolf Code*."

Darlene nodded and started to walk over to the woman when Maria grabbed her arm. "Darlene," she whispered. "When she leaves, I need you to tell me what is going on."

She nodded back, unsure of what to say. The woman kept glancing at Maria with confusion sweeping over her delicate features. Darlene introduced herself. The woman shook her hand.

"I'm Liara," she said to Darlene with her eyes still on Maria. "I'm a friend of Idris'. My husband left a book here for me."

Lucian's wife, Darlene realized with a jolt. She glanced behind her but Maria retreated into her office, the door locking firmly afterward. *Strange*, she thought, but relieved at the same time.

"Yes," she replied, turning back to Liara. "He did leave a book here."

Liara's eyes scanned across the bookstore now. "Oh my…what happened here?"

"We had a break-in last night. I'll try to find the book for you, okay? I'm sorry we're so disorganized."

"No, it's okay. I'm sorry to hear someone broke into your shop. That's horrible, truly."

Darlene looked around the shop in search of the oversized book. She knew Vivica left without it, but she wasn't sure where it ended up in the fight with Idris. She repeated her search in the supernatural section again, hoping it was still in the area.

"Did anyone get hurt?" Liara asked.

"My friend is missing."

"That's horrible!"

Darlene found the book wedged in between two similar sized books. She yanked it up from the floor and brought it over to Liara. Her face relaxed when she saw it.

Liara trailed her fingers over the cover and looked up at her. "My husband. Did he say anything when he gave it to you?"

"Just that someone would be coming by to pick it up."

Liara nodded, glancing around the bookstore again. "You, uh, know Idris well?"

"We're good friends," Darlene said, unsure of how to phrase it because she wasn't even sure where she stood with Idris.

"Well, I appreciate your help very much."

Liara nodded and glanced over at Maria's office again before leaving the shop, her high heels clicking loudly against the wood floor. The door closed behind her, and Darlene watched her go.

"Darlene?"

She turned around to see Maria peeking out from her office. "Yeah?"

"Can we talk?"

Darlene nodded and walked into the office.

<<<>>>

Idris headed down the street to Darlene, tossing around what Julie said to him. It didn't make sense. Julie rarely made sense. She was turned into a werewolf at the age of ten by a rabid group of werewolves down south. They tortured her for days until finally turning her. The pack then abandoned her. Julie had to figure everything out about being a werewolf on her own. She met Roman when she turned nineteen. The two of them had been together on and off since then.

Julie was strong and had been through a lot. But she was prone to heavy bouts of substance abuse. Her mind wasn't all there, and she would spout a lot of crazy stuff. Idris had to stop thinking about it.

Down ahead on the sidewalk, he could see Liara. She clutched *The Werewolf Code* to her chest, taking long strides through the tourists crowding the sidewalk. She was focused with her mouth set in a determined line. When she saw him, she gave a small wave and walked over to him.

"Where are you heading?" she asked.

"The bookshop. Everything go okay?"

A strange look crossed her face. "Why didn't you tell me?"

"Tell you what?"

"An Exsul is working in the shop."

Idris' heart suddenly pounded. An Exsul…there was no way Darlene was a werewolf. He would have sensed it instantly. His throat felt dry.

"What? Darlene?"

"No, her boss. The older woman… Maria."

Idris shook his head. "Maria isn't an Exsul. No way. I would have picked up on that instantly. How could I miss a werewolf? On top of that, an Exsul?"

Exsuls were exiled werewolves. They had no pack and ran alone. There were various reasons one became an Exsul, and none of them were good. Idris would have sensed a werewolf as soon as he had entered that bookshop. Maria didn't give off any werewolf signals at all.

"She hides it with magic… but I know. She knew I could tell and hid in the office."

"Doesn't it mean that Maria knows I am a werewolf too?"

Silence hung between them, and Idris felt his heart beat faster.

"Roman said the book was for him," he told Liara. "That Lucian was going to give up the pack to him."

Liara's face paled. "What?"

"What if Lucian knew about Maria? What if he left it in her shop with another werewolf so it could be protected?"

"Idris, what aren't you telling me about my husband?"

"A lot." Idris walked away now, hurrying to the bookshop. "I'll have to explain later."

<<◇>>

Darlene shut the door behind her and looked at Maria. She sat behind her desk with a tired expression. Her large glasses covered most of her face, and her white hair stuck up at funny angles. Her jewelry today was entirely lizard themed for some strange reason, and her shirt was a dark red that didn't match her yellow skirt. Darlene sat down across from her, wondering if she was going to get fired.

"Darlene," she said slowly. "I made a conscious effort to steer clear of inter-pack politics. When Lucian contacted me and told me about dropping off *The Werewolf Code* here until someone can come get it, I said fine. But I didn't want to know why he decided to relinquish the book and who would come to get it."

"Wait, what?"

"When Idris came by, I assumed he would get the book and leave. But I was wrong. He hung around and you began a relationship with him." Darlene began to speak, looking defensive. Maria held up a thin hand. "Don't. I've seen how you two look at each other. And now my shop is in ruins, and Lucian's wife came to collect the book. I should have put a stop to this earlier."

Darlene opened her mouth to speak again but her head was spinning. Nothing Maria said made sense. She was going to answer when the door to Maria's office burst open. Idris stood in the doorway. His eyes fell on Maria.

"Get away from her, Exsul," he growled at her.

"So Lucian's wife told you already?"

Darlene's gaze bounced between the two of them. "What is going on? What is an Exsul?"

"So what did you do to get banned from the packs, Maria? What did you do so badly that you were marked an Exsul? Let me see the tattoo… do you have the tattoo? Or are you using magic to block that as well so that no one else will know that you're an Exsul?"

Maria went stock still. Darlene looked at them both in confusion. *What is an Exsul? Does that mean Maria is…?*

"If you're an Exsul, why did you have *The Werewolf Code* here?" Idris continued. "Are you involved with what Lucian is planning?"

"Lucian was giving up the pack," Maria said stiffly. "He was going to become an Exsul as well. You know if you give up the book and dismantle the pack, the leader becomes an Exsul. He came to me, another Exsul, to keep it safe for whomever came to take it."

"Enough!" Darlene snapped and stood up, glaring at both of them. "Now both of you tell me what an Exsul is! I am not going to sit here and be left in the dark like this."

Idris crossed his arms and stared at Maria, who sighed. "Exsul is an exiled werewolf. We have no pack. We have no voice in pack affairs or anything affecting movements as a whole. We must be alone for the rest of our lives."

"You're a *werewolf*? Are you serious? This whole time?"

"Yes. I turned when I was fifteen. I became an Exsul ten years ago."

"Why?"

Maria shook her head. "I'm not talking about that. Not now. And especially not in front of *him*."

Idris grunted, "There isn't any good reason why a werewolf becomes an Exsul."

"My work is finished. Lucian's wife collected the book. My store is destroyed. There is nothing more I can give you or any of the other packs and nothing I care to give."

Darlene shook her head. She wasn't sure what to say. She wasn't even sure who to say it to. It was all too much. *Maria, her own boss, a werewolf? Was anyone around her normal? Was normal even a thing anymore?*

"You think you can just bow out now?" Idris said.

"I *am* bowing out now. I want nothing else to do with pack conflicts. I did what Lucian needed…"

They kept fighting. Their words swirled together and became one glob of noise that stuck to Darlene's ears. It seemed that everyone in her life was connected somehow to Lucian, and she didn't want to hear any more about it.

"That's it!" she yelled. "I don't want to hear from either one of you about this anymore."

She stormed out of the office, brushing against Idris who exclaimed, "Darlene?"

"No," she mumbled. "I shouldn't have gotten involved in this. What a nightmare this has become."

And she left the store behind, walking briskly to her car, hiding her torment. Darlene was grateful no one saw the tears falling down her face.

Chapter Twelve

Idris watched Darlene leave, a lump forming in his throat. He turned back to look at Maria, still sitting behind the desk, her expression unreadable.

"How come you didn't tell me you were one of us?"

"Why would I tell you? I would have to admit that I am an Exsul. It isn't as if you'd treat me with any respect because of it. Do the packs know that Darlene knows about them?"

He paused. "No."

"They'll be furious when they do, you know that, right? Especially because you didn't relocate or Change her. You'll be threatened with Exsul status by Lucian's wife."

"You're telling me things I already know."

Her eyes flashed. "You have Darlene wrapped up in things she shouldn't be wrapped up in. Now she knows about us and vampires and whatever else is going on."

"Did Lucian tell you why he was dismantling the pack?"

"No. He said he had something he wanted to try. Something that would make him an Exsul in the end."

"He wants to turn us into hybrids with vampires. Jacob, the worker you fired, who is missing — he's a vampire now. Do you know who changed him?"

Her face paled. "*Jacob?*"

"Darlene and I saw him at *Roman's Tavern*. Vivica, the vampire involved with Lucian, didn't admit to turning him. I know her, and she would have claimed it instantly. That means someone else did it."

Maria shook her head. "I don't know who turned that poor boy, but it's disgusting. The packs are disgusting and so are the vampires."

"Funny you should say that. Liara said you're using magic to block yourself from other werewolves. That's why I didn't notice you. So who is the witch that you convinced to help you?"

"None of your business." She stood up suddenly. "You need to leave. Leave Darlene alone if you know what's good for you. I'm an Exsul. Whatever happens with your pack doesn't interest me. But know this, Idris. If you don't figure out what you're doing, you'll be an Exsul yourself. You toed the line close for most of your life. Oh, don't look so surprised. I know about you. I know your anger and your rage at being a werewolf. I know how close you were to being tried for murdering that boy Brent. I wanted Darlene to find someone to make her happy after Austin cheated on her with a man, but not with you. Now get out."

Numbly, Idris turned around, thinking about what Maria said. He didn't know that Austin had left Darlene for another man. It explained why she was still hung up on him. Maybe he wasn't any better than Austin. Maybe Maria was right.

He stepped outside of the shop. The sun was setting, a brisk wind blew his way. Darlene's car was gone already. He shoved his hands in his pockets and stared out at the skyline. He wasn't sure what to do next. He had hit a dead end. Idris understood now what Lucian was trying to do — an idea that he believed in so much that he was willing to turn Exsul for it. Liara could lead the pack just fine. But could she survive what her husband was doing?

Rebecca was still out there, a feral vampire who had Vivica as her creator. Jacob was out there, too, turned by who knows. Lucian, plotting and planning with Vivica. Roman, who killed Brent without a second thought and would be extremely upset to know he had lost possible pack control already to Liara. And Julie's warning.

He had a bad feeling he couldn't shake.

Darlene drove around for a while, in an aimless way that she hadn't done in ages. She needed to figure out what to do next. She even considered packing up her things and moving away. She had enough in savings to get out of town and forget about all of this, like a bad dream. She was foolish to think she could help Idris.

The whole situation was nothing but bad news, and it only got worse from here on out.

She ended up in her apartment parking lot. With a sigh, she got out of the car and walked toward her apartment. What she wanted was a long hot shower followed by maintaining a vegetative state on her couch, wrapped up in blankets and watching TV. She couldn't think of anything else that sounded as lovely as that did.

It all happened so fast.

Darlene heard a twig snap behind her. Turning around, all she saw was a blur and then her back was pressed against the side of the apartment building, away from the light. Her breath caught in surprise, and she could feel iron tighten around her wrists. With a gasp, Darlene realized she was staring directly at Jacob.

"Darlene," he mumbled.

"Jacob, what are you doing here?"

"I had to come get you. My Maker wants to meet you."

"Are you crazy? I'm not going with you."

Darlene tried to wiggle away and out of his grip, but it was as if she was chained to the wall. His strength was more than she could even understand. He seemed amused and watched her attempt to break free of his grip. He wore the same clothes as the night she saw him at *Roman's Tavern*.

"You don't have any choice."

Something hit her hard on the head and all Darlene saw was darkness.

Idris called Darlene twice but there was no answer. He told himself to stop calling her because it was clear she wanted to be left alone. But the nagging feeling in his stomach grew. He looked out the motel window, unsure of where to go next. Liara had texted him, demanding the full story of why the book had been with an Exsul. He knew he had to tell her the truth. Idris recalled how much she cried when she found out Lucian went missing. Now he would have to tell her that her husband was a madman, too. He cursed and threw on his jacket. He set out to head over to Darlene's place.

Idris swung open the door and found himself staring at Liara. Her hair was down and falling across her shoulders in a black sheet. She had an oversized jacket on that Idris recognized as Lucian's.

"You didn't answer my text," she said by way of greeting.

"I have to see Darlene."

"Fine, but I'm coming with you. And I want you to tell me what is going on. I'm…pack leader now." Her voice caught at the end, as if she didn't believe it.

Idris didn't feel like arguing, "Fine. Let's go."

<<<>>>

Darlene drifted across the water. The sun beat down on her face. All around her was nothing but the ocean, quietly bobbing her along as she drifted. How did she get here? Her thoughts were slow and muddled, as if she was dreaming. Maybe she *was* dreaming. She couldn't remember the last thing she did.

Someone drifted by and called out to her. She turned her head to see a group of kids from grade school. Bullies. She was a pudgy kid, and they liked to make fun of her by pulling her pigtails and doing piggy noises. They floated by, calling out to her. Darlene ignored them.

There was someone else on the other side now. Austin. He was holding hands with his boyfriend. They were both in inner tubes, waving at her. Darlene felt rage engulf her. The rage was directed at Austin... at his lies... at the fact that he used her. But they paid no attention to her pain and then they were gone.

"I know what you are."

That deep voice, husky and dark, as if he was eating stones. Darlene looked above her and saw Idris, floating along his back as well.

"What I am?"

"You've always known, haven't you? From the books you've read. You just won't accept it."

"Accept what?"

"Your connection with things beyond this realm."

Darlene opened her mouth to reply but suddenly everything faded, and then there was only blackness around her.

Slowly, Darlene opened her eyes. The blackness crisscrossed with something. Trees, she realized. Stars dotted her vision, and she felt the dirt beneath her fingertips. She was outside.

"Oh good, you're awake." A soft, silky voice broke through the silence.

Darlene realized her head was tilted back against a tree trunk. She tried to move but her arms were tied around the trunk, her fingers brushing against the dirt. There was a man in front of her, walking slowly. His hair was messy, and his glasses glinted in the moonlight. She recognized him.

"Lucian."

"Nice to see you again."

Lucian walked over to her and crouched down. He was taller than she remembered. In the darkness, it was hard to make out his facial features. He walked with a gait that she didn't recognize from the store, as if he had been wounded. Fear gripped her as Darlene realized she was alone in the woods with him.

Lucian reached out and moved a strand of hair from her face, which made Darlene flinch. He laughed, a low laugh without any sort of humor in it.

"I thought I'd leave the book at your tiny shop for Roman and that would be that. I would do what I needed to do, be branded an Exsul if those narrow-minded fools decided upon it and have Roman take over the pack."

Darlene remained silent. She didn't want him to know his wife had come and gathered the book instead.

"But Idris was fast on my trail, trying to figure out where I had gone and why. By all accounts, nothing should have come out of his search for me." Lucian trailed his hand down to her wrist and squeezed just hard enough that tears sprung to Darlene's eyes. "But because of *you* and your interest in Brent, Idris never went away. And now you're here with me, and we're going to settle this tonight."

He stood up suddenly. Someone slunk out of the shadows. Jacob. He moved next to Lucian without a word and just smiled at Darlene.

"Prepare her. We've never tried this before and anything could happen."

Jacob's gaze flicked to Lucian briefly. "Master, you told me that I could be the one to drink the werewolf blood first."

Lucian waved his hand. "It will be so, but prepare her first. You're already a vampire. I'm sure you'll be able to successfully turn into a werewolf as well. We don't know what will happen with this one."

Panic surged through Darlene, and she struggled against the restraints as Jacob went over to her.

"Why are you doing this?" she finally gasped out through her fear.

"Because my Master knows the future. Vampires and werewolves as one creature. Imagine how we could rule the world. He's offering you an amazing chance, Darlene. You could become one of us. Rule with us."

"You're an idiot… the same idiot Maria had to fire. And he's an idiot, too, for this insane plan."

Lucian pushed Jacob out of the way with a low growl, crouching next to Darlene. Her palms felt sweaty, and her breathing was ragged as he stared her down.

"Did Idris explain what happens to people who find out about us? We either relocate them or we Change them."

"Idris said you always relocated them."

Lucian leaned in close and his breath moved against her ear. "I killed them." He backed his face away, staring at her again. "Idris didn't know. He didn't know a lot. He was too busy hating himself and everyone else for being a werewolf. I killed anyone who found out about us and told him we relocated them per the pack rules. Now I'm going to Change you. You're going to be our first human test subject to see if we can change you into the future." He stood up and looked down at Darlene in disgust. "Jacob. Prepare her."

<<◇>>

As they pulled into the parking lot of Darlene's apartment complex, Liara dabbed at her eyes with a tissue from her purse.

"I don't understand any of this," she said. "How could Lucian want to give the pack to Roman? Become Exsul? Try this stupid hybrid thing out?"

Idris shook his head. "I don't know, Liara. His motivations don't make sense to me. It doesn't seem like the man we both knew."

She brushed the tears from her eyes. "Let's go find your friend."

Idris tapped his fingers along the steering wheel. "Did you…did you pick up on anything with Darlene? Something odd?" At Liara's questioning gaze, Idris spoke again, "Julie mentioned that she was different…"

Liara scoffed, "Julie's different."

She got out of the truck without another word. Idris followed. He saw Darlene's car in the spot ahead of them and walked over to it. Nothing appeared out of place. Was he being stupid? She was probably in her apartment, safe and sound. Liara walked along the sidewalk, scanning the ground. Idris ran his fingers through his hair and was about to tell Liara that they should go back when she called him over.

He walked over to where she stood, against the side of the building, almost near the back, and she held something in her hand.

"What is it?"

Liara held out her hand. Darlene's cellphone. The screen was cracked down the center, the cracks branching out like spider webs along the glass screen.

Idris' heart lurched. "I'm going to follow the scent."

"You're going to Change *here*?"

"Something bad has happened. Are you going to come as well?"

"Alright, but I'm sending a text out for back up."

"To who, Liara? Roman's pack? We can't call our own. They're too far away and we can't trust Roman."

She paused for a moment and then shook her head. "Go. Change. Find her. I'll be right behind you."

Idris didn't wait another second. As he ran toward the forest behind Darlene's apartment building, he welcomed the Change. He felt his fingers elongate, the claws forming, his back hunching and legs shifting position. As he burst into the woods following Darlene's scent, he fought the urge to let out a howl to let whoever was with Darlene know that he was coming.

Jacob had Darlene lying on a slab of concrete with strange symbols gouged into it. There were shapes that depicted vampires and werewolves. Her arms were tied to a trunk above the slab but her feet were loose. She kicked and struggled but the ropes were too tight to break free. Behind her, Jacob and Lucian talked in low tones.

"The process is different for this one. She's entirely human. We don't even know if it will work," Lucian said.

"Let me drink your blood, Master. Let me see if I can complete the transition. This human will most likely die anyway, and we have nothing to fear. We're just going to see what goes wrong."

I have to get out of here. There has to be something I haven't thought of yet. Her eyes scanned the woods around her. Moonlight broke through the trees at some spots, shining down onto the ground. There was no way whatever they were planning would work on her. Jacob was right. She was going to die.

She heard a soft noise and slurping sounds as Jacob drank from Lucian. Lucian chanted something, some sort of spell, Darlene assumed. She controlled her breathing. They were distracted now and this was her only chance to escape. Darlene slowed down her breathing and closed her eyes. Her dream from before floated back to her. She was on the ocean... Idris telling her something was trying to break through to her — her connection with another realm — was it just dream gibberish? She recalled what she saw in the woods that one night, floating, ghost-like.

I've always known, she thought, sending her thoughts out around her. *Please, now I need you to help me.*

She opened her eyes. Behind her, Jacob made a strange choking noise but she couldn't see what was going on. In front of her, however, a shape formed out of a cloud of mist. Darlene focused on it to make it take shape, but mist was all she could bring to it. Her mind was exhausted even doing this little to the spirit in front of her.

I saw you, the night in the woods. My fear made you come into focus, didn't it? You're a ghost. I'm not powerful enough to hear what you're saying to me. But if you can hear me, please loosen my ties.

A shape ran past her — Jacob, toppling into the bushes, away from view. There was gurgling and terrible noises in the bushes as Jacob tried to Change into a hybrid. Darlene focused again on the spirit in front of her. Her head pounded as the mist wafted over her, dousing her in what felt like cold water.

Lucian slid into view. "I'm afraid Jacob is too ill to help us for this next part. It'll be just the two of us to witness your historic transformation."

Darlene sensed the ties around her wrists loosen from an unseen force. She barely paid any attention to Lucian as she kept her focus on the spirit. The ties fell gently to the ground, freeing her hands.

Thank you.

Darlene broke her focus on the spirit, and it faded away. Lucian came toward her, a knife raised, a crazed look over his face as Darlene slid her fingertips around a blade at the edge of the concrete slab. He raised the knife and at the same time Darlene lunged forward, slamming the blade into his chest.

Lucian let out a scream and stumbled back in surprise, his eyes wide. Darlene slid off the concrete slab as Lucian took another step back. She heard something crashing through the woods now, loud and vicious. Jacob had gone still in the bushes.

Then two werewolves burst through on the opposite side of the clearing.

Idris looked around the clearing, trying to understand what he was seeing. There was an altar with strange carvings. Lucian stood over it, clutching at his chest. Darlene stood nearby him, looking at Idris with wide-eyes. Liara let out a whimper and stepped toward Lucian. Idris nudged Liara back with his snout. She wasn't nearly as large as he was in werewolf form but she was faster. Liara dodged him before darting by Darlene's side and transforming back into human form quickly. Liara always had better control over her emotions than Idris.

Idris wanted to Change back but was momentarily stunned by what he saw. Lucian let out a gurgle and hit the ground on his knees. Blood bloomed out from around the blade that protruded from his chest. Idris felt time slow down.

"Oh my god," Darlene said. "He was going to — I just needed him to — I don't..." She looked stricken.

"Lucian!" Liara ran over and crouched in front of him, cupping his face in her hands. "I'm here now! It's okay. I'm here!"

"Liara…"

"It's okay. I found the book. I'm pack leader now. I won't make you Exsul. We can forget about all of this." She was crying now — Idris saw her shoulders shaking.

"You?" Lucian rasped. "No…no…Roman…"

"Lucian?"

There was another movement in the bushes and Darlene screamed a second too late. Something flew out of the bushes, faster than Idris had even seen before and slammed into him. He flew through the air and smashed against a tree, the wind knocked out of him. He let out a deep growl and leapt to his feet again, but could only stare at what was in front of him.

Jacob stood in front of him, but he wasn't a vampire any longer. His fangs were exposed, and his eyes turned a red color but his arms were disfigured, having the terrible claws of a werewolf. His feet were the same. Hair sprouted all over his body in random spots, at odds with his pale vampire skin.

A hybrid.

Jacob looked like a werewolf stuck in mid-Change. Idris pushed off with his hind legs, snarling and lunged at Jacob but he was gone in a flash. He reappeared behind Idris to sink his fangs into the werewolf's leg.

Idris lost his footing and stumbled to the ground, kicking up dirt in an attempt to get Jacob off of him.

"No!" Darlene ran over toward them.

Idris howled at her, signaling for her to leave. Liara laid Lucian's body down, a pool of blood underneath him. Jacob spun and grabbed Darlene by the throat, lifting her up into the air.

"What did you do to him?" Jacob screamed in a distorted voice. "What powers do you have?"

"I don't—" Her breath cut off.

Idris took advantage of the distraction and ran into Jacob, slashing his claws and sinking his jaws into his side. Blood filled his mouth, and it tasted vile. Jacob dropped Darlene, who hit the ground with a thud. She rubbed her neck and gasped for air but was otherwise unharmed. Jacob spun and kicked Idris with his foot. His claws sliced into Idris, who let out a howl and fell back. He was Changing back — how could that be?

Jacob let out a low chuckle. "I have more powers than you will ever understand," he spat, glancing around the clearing. "I'm not done, do you understand?"

Idris felt his paws Changing back into human hands, his body slowly losing its fur and his snout morphing back into his proper face. Jacob ran past him and into the woods. Idris wanted to chase him, to get him back, but he could feel the wounds along his stomach oozing blood. Darlene appeared above him.

"He's gone." Her face was tear-stained. "Idris, hang in there! Idris!"

But darkness overtook him.

Chapter Thirteen

Darlene didn't like being with Roman's pack. They showed up right after Idris passed out. Liara had called them as back-up, but the danger, for the moment, had passed. Roman stumbled in on Liara crying over Lucian's dead body and Darlene tried to shake Idris awake. The pack had swooped in and taken everyone back to their pack headquarters, which was a warehouse just outside of town.

Now Darlene was lying in a makeshift hospital room, watching Idris sleep. She wanted him to go to the hospital, but Liara said that they always tended to their own. Someone had patched Idris up and now his chest was covered in heavy bandages. He was heavily medicated and sleeping soundly.

She felt dirty, gross and terrible. She kept staring at her hands, wracked with feelings of guilt from killing Lucian and relief that it wasn't her that was killed instead.

There was a spirit. She didn't make that up. Jacob had sensed something was off too. Darlene had seen a ghost in the woods the night Vivica and Idris fought. Her recent dreams hinted at it as well. She was always attracted to stories of ghosts and spirits, but she assumed that was her own creepy interests and nothing that indicated a power inside of her.

How could she have this power inside of her and know absolutely nothing about it? She chewed on her bottom lip, mulling it over. They were going to ask. They would ask how she freed herself. What would she say?

"Hey."

Darlene looked up at the whisper. Liara had pushed back the sheet that made up the door to Idris' recovery room. She had Lucian's blood on her clothes and her makeup was smudged from crying. Darlene wasn't sure if she was going to attack her for murdering her husband.

"Hi, Liara."

"Mind if I come in?"

"No, of course not."

Liara stepped inside and walked over to Idris' bedside, looking down at him. "The doctor said he'll be okay. Just needs to rest. I need to talk to you."

Darlene nodded and Liara came over to sit next to her on the couch they had put in the room.

"A lot is going on. Idris told me what he discovered. And that you know about us. And vampires. In a case like this where the pack leader is missing, Idris should have followed procedure. Relocation or Change.

Nothing else. He's facing Exsul status because he failed to do either."

Darlene's heart skipped a beat. "What? No. Don't give him Exsul status. It's my fault. He didn't want to Change me, and I refused relocation. I wanted to help him. What was he supposed to do? The only other option would have been to kill me. Lucian didn't relocate anyone. He told me he killed them."

Liara shut her eyes briefly, and Darlene wondered if she had gone too far. "I am the pack leader now. I understand what my husband did and that he would become Exsul for it. But I need you to tell me what happened, and spare nothing regarding my own feelings for my husband."

Darlene nodded and told her what happened with Lucian and Jacob.

Idris' eyes fluttered open. The first thing he felt was pain… all over. He grunted and clutched at his stomach, remembering what had happened. Jacob. The first werewolf-vampire hybrid. He had kicked Idris' ass and was now out there, somewhere, free.

And Lucian was dead.

"You up?"

Idris looked toward where the voice came from. Julie stood in front of a sheet. He realized with a start that he was at Roman's pack headquarters. Julie looked terrible, wearing clothes that were too big for her and dark circles around her eyes.

"Hear about your girlfriend?"

"Is she okay?"

"Oh, she's fine. But she's exactly what I told you... a ghost walker."

Idris' head ached. "Can you please get out?"

Julie sneered, "I done warned you, pup."

As Julie slid out of the room, Liara stepped in. Their eyes met briefly. "Hey, how are you feeling?"

"Been better. You going to tell me what's going on? Where's Darlene?"

"I sent Darlene home."

"You what? She's a target. By Vivica, Rebecca, Jacob, and who knows who else!"

"I sent Mark with her as a guard. She'll be okay. I just needed to talk to you."

Idris looked at her. "What? How bad is it?"

Liara paced the room, talking the entire time, explaining what had happened in the woods from her standpoint, as well as Darlene's. When she finished the debriefing, she stopped pacing and looked at Idris.

"You mean to tell me Darlene has some sort of...otherworldly power?"

"Yes, that's right. She didn't know about it until recently. I think communicating with our world has brought it out in her."

Idris sank back in the pillows. "Now what?"

"You're facing Exsul status, Idris. But with Darlene's powers, I can try to get the pack to side with you on it... that she is one of us... not a mere human. Therefore her knowledge of us will be tolerated. But, like you said, Roman is furious about the fact the book is in my hands and not his. He wants you to be Exsul. He's pushing for it. And you know all packs in the area weigh in on all decisions regarding Exsul status."

"Yes, I know." He closed his eyes.

"I'll do what I can. But we have bigger problems. Jacob is still alive. From what I can gather, Lucian turned him to a vampire. But how? And now we have a hybrid on our hands."

"We don't know if he can even live in that state. He could just die out there in the woods."

Liara nodded. "I sincerely hope so."

Darlene looked out the window of her apartment. The sun burned high in the sky but she still felt jumpy. Even with Mark posted outside her door, she felt nervous. Mark was still part of Roman's pack. She saw Roman's face when he found out that Liara possessed the book and had taken over as pack leader instead of him. He was furious. Why would one of his own protect her?

Liara advised Darlene to lay low for a while because of her story and her direct involvement in killing Lucian. So it was back to being a hermit. Her phone was still out of commission but she didn't feel like repairing it right away. She wanted to sleep for a long time and hopefully wake up to find out this was all a bad dream.

Darlene heard low voices at the door, and her heart stopped for a moment. Then the apartment door opened and she saw Mark.

"Idris is here. I can get rid of him if you want. I would love to do it, personally."

"No, no, it's fine. Let him in."

"No fun," Mark said.

Idris moved past him, and the two glared at each other until Mark shut the door. *Like we have time for pissing contests.* Idris moved slowly, the pain written all over his face as he sat down on the couch across from Darlene. She remained sitting in front of her computer. She could see the bandages under his shirt.

"How are you feeling?"

"Been better. You?"

"The same."

Silence filled the room until Idris cleared his throat. "I heard about…about the ghost thing."

"Everyone is expecting me to have all these answers, but I don't have any. I just knew there was a spirit there. In desperation, I called for it. It took no form at all. It was just mist. And now everyone thinks I can raise the dead or something and I just —"

"Hey, hey." Idris stood up and walked over to her side, wiping tears from her face. "It's okay. We'll figure it out together."

"You're facing Exsul status because of me, Idris. I should have listened to you and gone away somewhere. I'm so sorry."

Idris crouched in front of her, his eyes warm and kind. "Stop, Darlene. I told you, we'll figure it out together."

"But Jacob is still out there."

"The threat of the hybrid monsters or whatever Lucian called them has passed for now, okay? Jacob doesn't have his Maker anymore. It's a big blow. We have time to regroup before we have to worry about anything… plenty of time to figure out what is going on with you, okay?"

Darlene sniffled. "You mean it?"

"I mean it."

Idris tilted her face up to his, leaned down and kissed her. Her despair washed away. The warmth that

Idris could always bring came over her, slowly and sweetly. Darlene felt her heart rate lower as he kissed her.

"I know we're both wounded," he whispered. "Literally and emotionally. But I want to be with you, Darlene… if you'll have me."

Darlene smiled back. "I'll have you."

It was silly, given all that happened so far, but for the first time in a long time, even though everything else was messy and crazy, she felt that her love life was back on track.

-To be continued in Book 2-

If you enjoyed this title, I would appreciate your leaving a review of the book. Good reviews encourage an author to write as well as help books to sell. Good reviews can be just a few short sentences describing what you liked about the book without having a spoiler. If you could spend 30 seconds writing a review, I would appreciate it: you can review this title right now at your favorite retailer.

Here is a preview of the **next story** you may also enjoy:

Alpha Packed: A BBW Paranormal Shifter Romance - Book 2

AT FIRST there was only the hunger. It pulsed through Rebecca, tricking her into thinking she was actually alive. But she knew better than that, didn't she? She spent most of the night staring into a mirror, seeing nothing in the reflection… as if she had been wiped from the pages of the history books completely.

They were looking for her. She saw posters plastered around town, asking for any information on where she had gone since the bookshop was ransacked. She kept her head low and chopped off most of her hair in exchange for the semblance of a normal hairstyle. She had gone back to try and find her friend, Darlene.

But the hunger clouded everything. It was too dangerous to talk to anyone. Then it became too dangerous to even stand near them. The smell of their skin, alive, with blood pumping just under the surface, was too much to bear. She had retreated into the woods.

Just as daylight approached, she stumbled across an empty cabin that overlooked the highway. Clawing at the floorboards, she managed to get herself into the ground before the sunlight could shine into the cabin.

Now it was the middle of the night and she was staring at the soulless mirror. She was almost glad she couldn't see herself. She didn't want to see herself. Because the mess behind her was already too gruesome. A hitchhiker had thought she could stay here the night as well…but she was fatally mistaken.

No, Rebecca didn't want to see herself in the mirror. She didn't need to, because she knew what the mirror would show. Her face, smeared red... her hands, coated in the hitchhiker's blood. Rebecca could just make out the girl's hand, sticking out from behind the makeshift bed, her fingers curled slightly, a slick pool of blood sliding out from underneath her body. It was her first feeding and she made a huge mess of it.

Rebecca closed her eyes and screamed.

"Am I under suspicion of anything?"

"No, ma'am."

"Truly? Because it honestly feels like you suspect me of something." Darlene crossed her arms and leaned back in the chair, staring down Officer Walsh. Normally, she had the utmost respect for police officers and knew Walsh was just doing his job. But she couldn't help but think of him as a pain in the ass.

"Listen, Miss Troop, I'm just trying to understand why you went to see Ms. Boots that night."

"And I told you a thousand times already. I tried to make you guys aware of the forum post by her son that I found. I was blown off here, so I went to his mother directly to tell her."

"I just don't understand why you're involved in an old case from someone who has no connection with you whatsoever."

"Why does it matter? I didn't murder her, and it feels like you're suggesting I did. Do I need to get a lawyer?"

Walsh paled. "No, there's no need for that, ma'am. They're just routine questions. What did Ms. Boots say when you went to her with your information?"

"She told me she had known already that he thought he was a werewolf. She told me that he fell in with the wrong crowd. She was very sad about it all. But she confirmed that someone picked Brent up that night. So my information was useless, like the cops said. Brent's mother already knew that someone came for him that night."

Darlene hoped her story sounded convincing. Most of the details were true. It was just the circumstances of the details that were fudged a little.

Walsh looked down at his notepad. "What about *Roman's Tavern*? Witnesses put you there last week. Your boyfriend got into a fight with Roman. No cops were called, and the two of you bailed afterward, from my understanding."

Darlene's heart thrummed. For a second, she wanted to shake Idris. Why in the world did he fight with Roman that night? Of course people would have seen them and word would have gotten back to the police. It was a vicious fight. She didn't know that Walsh had heard about the fight already though. Who blabbed?

"So?"

"So if Roman decides to press charges, your boyfriend will be in a lot of trouble."

"As far as I know, Roman didn't press charges. So what is the question?"

"Why were you at *Roman's Tavern* that night?"

"I can't go to a bar with my boyfriend?"

Walsh leaned forward. "I just find it strange that after I mentioned to you that Jacob was interested in going to *Roman's Tavern* that you ended there as well. And you seemed so interested in Brent Boot's death, that he had a connection to *Roman's Tavern* as well."

Darlene felt warm. She didn't like lying to the police. But it wasn't as if they would believe the truth anyway. *Well, the truth is, my boyfriend is a werewolf. His pack leader wanted to exile himself from the werewolves in order to craft a werewolf-vampire hybrid creature. No, don't worry – he's dead! Yeah, I killed him with the help of a spirit. Yes, I said spirit. Turns out, I have power over ghosts that no one understands, myself included. Jacob is a hybrid and is out there somewhere doing God only knows what. My best friend is a missing vampire, and her Maker is a crazy bitch. You are chasing leads that go nowhere because my insane social circle, including my werewolf Exsul boss, is on the case!*

Ugh. It sounded like a terrible anime.

"This is just a questioning, right?" When Walsh nodded, Darlene stood up. "Then I'm done for the day.

I have to get to work. The bookstore re-opens tomorrow. Where are you on my missing friend, by the way… while you sit here and accuse me of murder?"

"No one is accusing you of anything, Miss Troop. We don't have any leads on your friend yet. Has she been in touch with you?"

"No," Darlene said, trying to keep the sadness out of her voice. "I'm leaving now."

Walsh shook his head as Darlene left the room. It felt as if every cell in her body was vibrating slightly, making her head hurt. She dreaded this police station now. Why did she ever try to tell them about Brent and his forum post? It just ended up biting her in the ass.

As she stepped out into the sunlight and slid a pair of sunglasses on, she thought of Rebecca. Still no sign of her. Darlene was hoping Rebecca would try to call her. She kept thinking back to Rebecca opening her eyes and bursting out of the room, into the night. Guilt immersed heavily in her heart. Idris warned her that newborn vampires were feral and dangerous. Usually their Makers remained nearby to help guide them through their ordeal. But Vivica had no interest in taking care of Rebecca.

Darlene got in her car, ignoring whispers from a couple of teenagers nearby. She knew they were talking about her negatively, making remarks on her weight. *I don't care. I'm above this shit.* If she repeated it enough times, maybe it would finally sink in.

She looked at her phone and saw a text from Idris. He asked how the meeting with Walsh went. Darlene paused, unsure of what to type. She was touched that he had texted her with everything else going on in his world. *My boyfriend.* The phrase seemed so foreign to her. How could Idris, such an imposing, strong and sexy werewolf, be dating her, of all people?

Darlene lectured herself again. She deserved this. She deserved to have a boyfriend who made her happy, was great in bed and clearly interested in her. She had to stop trying to ruin herself and not let herself be happy. It was easier said than done. With a sigh, she typed out a reply. *Okay, but he is asking questions about why we were at Roman's Tavern the night we saw Jacob. What about your end?*

She sent the text and pulled out of the parking lot, heading toward the bookshop. She had been putting in extra hours since the time Lucian had tried to kill her to turn her into a hybrid. Originally, Darlene was furious with Maria for keeping the fact she was a werewolf a secret – an Exsul on top of that – but she understood more now why Maria did it. Darlene learned as much as she could about Exsuls in case Idris received that as his sentence. Plus working at the bookshop kept her busy, which meant no time for thinking about how she had killed Lucian.

No, do not go down that road, not right now. Darlene turned down the main street. She was almost at the bookshop. She would be busy soon.

If you enjoyed this sample then look for **Alpha Packed: A BBW Paranormal Shifter Romance - Book 2**.

Here is a preview of **another story** you may also enjoy:

Alpha Feud: A BBW Paranormal Shifter Romance - Book 1

"Breaking news: A body has been found in the woods outside the town of Lancaster over the weekend. The county coroner has noted the cause to be what looks like an animal attack.

Sources say there have been sightings of 'wolf-like' creatures found in the area that may or may not be responsible, according to investigators. This is the third unsolved case of this nature that has been reported in the region."

ELIZA TUGGED at the zipper of her wind poncho in an attempt to cover her exposed skin. The wind was getting more fierce and it was still raining, but her network manager believed that rain added to the 'drama' of a broadcast. *Drama? What kind of 'drama' could there possibly be from covering a livestock contest?*

Of course, Eliza would never challenge her boss's choices to his face. Jim was a well-respected man in their town and, in fact, could be regarded as the biggest local celebrity. Jim used to work as an anchor in a major Los Angeles broadcasting station, but had chosen to return to Birkbridge and start his own broadcasting company. They had started off small but had managed to accumulate a decent following of loyal viewers and had therefore been able to expand into a full-fledged TV and radio station.

Under Jim's influence, Eliza had lived for a long time in a state of bedazzlement. After all, she had, once upon a time, fallen in love with the world of Jim's creation. Jim and his television station - Birkbridge NewsLine - had brought some sense of excitement to the otherwise boring little town. The problem was that, after five years of working for the man, she'd learned to see through the sparkly shades of spectacle. Once the illusion had shattered, the outcome was quite depressing; Eliza was, once more, living in the real world.

For people like Eliza's boyfriend, Andrew Freelander, 'normal' was not synonymous with boring. He was a man of simple pleasures and routine; he enjoyed his black coffee in the mornings and his beers in the evenings. Every other day, he went to shoot some pool at the local pub with his friends and colleagues from the weapons factory. Sometimes Eliza joined, sometimes she didn't. She didn't plan ahead most of the time, because she didn't want her entire life to be dominated by routine. Thanks to Jim, she felt as if her life might change for a while and become at least a little less monotonous. However, after many years, Eliza's new and 'exciting' life became its own routine.

And at the moment, she stood in front of a farm, reporting on an upcoming livestock show in the pouring rain. *Yippidy yay.*

"And now, reporting from the Birkbridge countryside farm: a soaked and very cold cow!" Eliza shouted into the camera.

Oliver, the cameraman, rolled his eyes. "Thank God we're not filming live television!" he yelled at her through the roaring wind. "And I don't see any cows around here, but I'm so bloody tired of not doing my job today that I might just be hallucinating!"

The wind was finally dying down and Oliver was pointing his camera at Eliza again. "None of that "cow" nonsense this time, Eliza! The people of this town are paying good money to get their news from a real human woman."

"You make a good point." Eliza smiled. Oliver was a good sport; he was the only British person in Birkbridge, and he certainly knew how to have a good bit of banter. Eliza decided to cut him some slack and snap into work mode; she knew that the rain might start again in a few seconds so they needed to get the shot right then and there.

"This is Eliza Zachary, reporting from the soon-to-be Birkbridge livestock fair. As you can see, preparations are under way for the upcoming festivities…"

Whenever she did stories like this, Eliza couldn't help but wonder what it would've been like if she'd accepted the job offer in Boston. The job had initially seemed way beyond her reach, but her father had pulled some strings with a few of his contacts at the news station and managed to convince Eliza to apply. To her amazement, she had been immediately accepted for the role of an on-site broadcasting journalist. Pursuing the job in Boston would have allowed Eliza to do what she'd always wanted and follow in the footsteps of her father. Granted, she wouldn't be on any real battlefront, but she would still be in the position to make history with her news stories. However, taking the job in Boston would also have prevented her from continuing her happy life with Andrew, her loving, loyal boyfriend.

Andrew and Eliza first met in their first year of college and had been inseparable ever since. She believed that Andrew was the only person, other than her dad, who she could truly be herself around. Although they didn't exactly have an instant connection, Eliza and Andrew grew close in a very natural way, and their relationship developed with ease. Before starting her first year of Media Studies, Eliza had promised herself that she would make an effort to interact with other people. College was meant to be the best time of her life, and Eliza wasn't about to let her insecurities get in the way of that. With some life coaching and advice from her dad and some styling tips from her mom, Eliza had fashioned her very own alter ego with which she would face the world head-on.

Through thick and thin, Eliza's father had always been her rock. Her mother, Jeanette, was always supportive, but she was sometimes a bit too fussy for Eliza to truly confide in her.

While growing up, Eliza had known her father as two men: the brave, effortlessly cool man who yelled over the sound of gunfire from the television screen, and the reserved, gentle man who tucked her into bed every night. Of course, the television Martin looked a lot different, since Eliza watched all his broadcasts as old recordings. By the time she was born, Martin had given up his career and settled down in Birkbridge to raise his family. He became a local historian, pursuing lengthy and in-depth projects relating to the foundational elements of Birkbridge life. These revolved around the three main industries in the town: coalmining, farming and manufacturing guns. His new book required him to research the inner workings of the Millstone Firearms factory, and he could often be found hanging out in the area, talking to some of the workers. Some of the workers didn't mind him, but others would sneer at him and ask him condescending questions. "Have you ever tried using Google, old man? You know we don't have all day to chat with you about your picture books."

Despite his seemingly old-fashioned methods and even though he was a bit of a social outcast, Martin was still unbelievably charming. Perhaps it was due to his immaculately well-preserved good looks, or maybe because of his patience and open-minded listening skills, but Martin's investigative projects usually bore fantastic results. He often took on paid projects for some extra cash. Sometimes, locals would hire him to investigate and produce their family trees. In other cases, his clients were people who wanted him to find anecdotes or even write entire biographies for their dead relatives' funerals. One thing was for sure; his clients were never disappointed.

Going along with her father's suggestion, Eliza joined the drama club and after five months, Eliza had had a decent amount of interaction with the club's one and only groupie; a cute senior named Andrew. At first, she was a little annoyed with his tendency to hang around and watch their practices. Eliza was new to this scene and still felt a bit self-conscious, particularly around people who weren't even part of the theater group. For this reason, Andrew's casual presence had frustrated her a little bit. Who was this guy? Didn't he have anything better to do?

The first time that Eliza found herself alone with Andrew, she had been unexpectedly upfront with him. She was usually shy around guys, but she found him so *annoying* that her frustration managed to surpass her bashfulness. Although sarcasm hadn't been part of her repertoire at the time, Eliza's first conversation with Andrew was loaded with it.

"Haven't seen you in a while," she'd said with a cheeky grin on her face. "You must've been really busy lately."

Andrew had been at their practices every single day that week, so he laughed at her ironic insinuations that he had no life. And, as it turned out, Andrew had liked Eliza's direct approach to conversation. Due to her former friendlessness, Eliza hadn't really learned how to engage in small talk and empty chitchat; she was an all-or-nothing kind of girl. Andrew, as an attractive college senior, had become accustomed to empty, flirtatious interactions with the opposite sex. However, Andrew was a self-proclaimed monogamist and he quickly tired of the attention overload. Throughout college, he'd been looking to settle down, but to his dismay, all the co-eds seemed the same to him; he never found anyone amongst his groupies who really challenged him the right way. So Andrew became a groupie himself and started hanging out with the drama club. As he explained to Eliza, he was looking to find some truth in the fiction of theater. Eliza had rolled her eyes and called him a cheeseball. Then they exchanged looks, Eliza's mouth twisting into a crooked smile, and they both burst into laughter.

Andrew had been persistent, and had won Eliza over within two weeks. They'd hang out after the theater club practices, and their private meetings had escalated. At first, they met up in cafés, then bars, and eventually, Andrew's apartment. Quickly, Eliza and Andrew became in sync with one another, and there was no awkwardness in discussing their plans for the future. After she completed her sophomore year, Andrew asked Eliza to move in with him, and she gladly accepted.

Andrew had graduated three years earlier than Eliza and immediately got a job at Millstone Firearms. After five years his responsibilities had increased immensely. Despite his reputation for being late to almost everything, Andrew was nothing but exceptional at what he did, in fact, ever since Andrew received his promotion to junior head of sales, Millstone Firearms had managed to out-sell their competitors by ten percent annually, which meant that they were finally on their way to becoming the most successful firearms manufacturer in the country.

For Eliza, parting with Andrew hadn't really been an option. Since she hadn't, in her wildest dreams, expected that the Boston network would actually consider her application, let alone offer her a job, Eliza had been completely befuddled about how to act when she'd received the offer. Deep down, she had already known that Andrew would not be willing to give up his job and leave Birkbridge, and she also realized that he simply wouldn't be able to keep up with the pace of life in the east coast. After all, the only things that kept Andrew's absent-mindedness at bay were his routines and habits, but he was completely unable to adjust to changes in his schedule.

Nevertheless, Eliza had had a tiny speckle of hope when she confronted Andrew about her job offer. He had been incredibly sweet, kissing Eliza and telling her that he was so proud of her; after all, what were the odds for getting such an incredible job offer straight-out-of-college? However, the fantasy wasn't meant to last. After lengthy conversations over breakfast, dinner and weekend pillow talk, Andrew and Eliza eventually came to the sad yet inevitable conclusion that the move to Boston wasn't going to pan out. They both knew that Andrew had worked incredibly hard to achieve his current company status, and neither of them believed that he should have to start from square one again. They discussed the possibility of Eliza moving on her own, but her fully packed Boston work schedule would ultimately overrule the possibility of her flying out to see Andrew once every few months. For Andrew, given his recent promotion, the chances of taking time for visitation days were also very slim.

As Eliza helped Oliver pack up his camera equipment, she told herself that she had no regrets. In actuality, the decision to stay in Birkbridge with Andrew had been a no-brainer. She had been able to get everything she wanted: a loving boyfriend *and* a job. Granted, this job may not have been a first choice, but it was certainly not a job that anyone in their right mind could complain about.

Arriving home, Eliza checked the time on her phone, 6:29 pm, and in the process discovered several texts from Melissa, one of her three best friends and also, coincidentally, a cousin.

5:30: *Done with work, where are you right now?*

5:44: *Not gonna bother going home first, brought a change of clothes to work so heading to the bar now! Will see you there.*

6:08: *There's a hot guy here. Hurry or I'll go home with him!*

6:10: *Just kidding but seriously, get here already.*

When Eliza walked into *Nelly's*, Melissa was sitting at their usual spot. There were a few empty glasses already lined up at the table, but she was still looking relatively sharp. As Eliza knew from experience,

Melissa could be trusted to hold her liquor. Even on nights when she consumed triple the doses of her friends, Melissa would always be the last one standing.

Eliza took a seat opposite her friend. "So where's this dreamy guy? I was almost expecting you to be gone by the time I arrived."

"All kidding aside, if my vodka-goggles aren't deceiving me, I think there really *is* a somewhat hot guy here tonight. He's at the bar though, so be a doll and check him out for me while you're up there?"

Eliza rolled her eyes and sighed dramatically, but she couldn't stop herself from smiling. "Oh, all right then. But only because I love you."

"You're the best!" Melissa beamed, giving her friend an overly exaggerated wink. There was something about their weekly girly meet-ups that had spurred the friends to engage in a satirical 80's-housewife-routine.

Eliza came back from the bar, carrying two cocktails. "So, no sight of Brienne yet. Or has she also wondered off with some mystery man?"

"Yes. She's finally left boring old Tom and those dreadful kids and found herself a real man," Melissa responded, without breaking character.

At that moment, Brienne came through the door, dithering about as always. She wiped her feet on the carpet and, spotting the flaw of their seating arrangement, shuffled over to another table and grabbed a chair.

"Hey, sorry I'm so late, what did I miss?"

"Not much. Well, Melissa has spotted someone she thinks is hot, but that's about it," Eliza responded matter-of-factly.

"Ah, good, so I didn't miss anything," Brienne confirmed, slouching back on her chair and looking calm at last.

If you enjoyed this sample then look for **Alpha Feud: A BBW Paranormal Shifter Romance - Book 1**.

Here is a preview of **another story** you may also enjoy:

Star Bright, Book 1 by Carla Coxwell

THE SUNLIGHT creeps into my room. I groan and turn my head the other direction, trying to sleep through it. The last thing I feel like doing is getting up this morning. I never want to get up again. Everything I've done for the last few months has been robotic.

The holiday season is usually my favorite time of year. There is nothing I love more than browsing around the shops, looking for the best things to buy for my parents and friends.

That was before everything in my life went to hell. Now the thought of seeing anyone or even shopping makes me want to go back to sleep for the rest of the day.

Maggie… my daughter…

This would have been her first Christmas.

The thought comes to me quickly, before I can attempt to stop it. I try to stop all thoughts of her. Yet all it does is drive me into the pit of despair even faster. If I start thinking about her now, I will never get out of bed. I tell myself I will handle this morning the way I handle every other morning – with baby steps.

Open my eyes. It sounds ridiculous to make that a step but when I tell myself baby steps, I truly mean baby steps. If I think of what to do all at once – get up, shower, make coffee – it is all so overwhelming that I don't want to leave my bed.

The baby steps continue. Get out of bed. Walk to the bathroom. Brush my teeth. Open the shower door. Depression makes even the thought of getting in the shower to wash, only to do it all over again tomorrow, seem idiotic.

After my shower, I decide to go grocery shopping. I remember coming home last night and not finding anything substantial to eat. Instead I ate three slices of bread and went to bed. My stomach is growling loudly at me, demanding something decent to eat.

I slip on an oversized long-sleeved T-shirt and a pair of baggy jeans. Gone are the times when I cared about what I looked like. I don't want anyone to notice me ever again. It is safe to be by myself. I tell myself I can handle being alone.

Before I leave, I check my bank account on my phone. My savings are dwindling. I need to get a job. This can't last forever. When I quit my job, I figured something else would fall into my lap. But it's hard to have things fall in your lap when you never leave your bed. *I'm becoming pathetic.* I grab my purse and head out into the chilly morning.

A thin layer of snow covers the ground. The sun has now retreated behind a mass of gray clouds. They threaten a heavy snowfall. I wouldn't mind if it snowed everyone in. Sadly, Netflix is my new best friend.

The grocery store is brimming with families with their kids in tow, out of school for the holidays. I curse myself for not thinking of this before I left my apartment this morning. I wander around blindly, my list in hand, as my gaze falls on the kids around me. My heart beats quickly in my chest and my skin feels numb. All I want is to take Maggie's hand and walk through the store with her. I would kill to see her try to grab something off the shelf or plead with me to get her a doll in the small toy section.

Instead I am alone, a panic attack blooming on the brink. What is my trigger exactly? Happy kids? Couples who look down at their children and beam? I feel stupid as I park my basket in a random aisle and bolt into the restroom, which is thankfully empty. I go into one of the stalls then close my eyes tightly.

I can't live like this forever. Every time I decide to leave the house, I find myself overwhelmed by people or past memories. Everything seems to be trying to get my attention, telling me that my old dreams have died and I am letting life pass me by.

I have done things in my life that I am not proud of. I have terrible taste in men. I have a habit of only being attracted to assholes or drunks and I have had no issues cheating on people to be with someone else.

My skin feels hot and itchy as I try to avoid the panic attack that will knock me over. I focus on my breathing.

I am here. I am here. I am here.

I am nowhere else. What I have done in the past is in the past. I can't get Maggie back. I won't get Paul back after what I've done to him. I even feel like I deserve what Robbs has done to me.

Focusing on my breathing and repeating my mantra helps slow my heart rate down. I am glad no one else has come into the bathroom. The last thing I need is someone else thinking I am crazy.

After ten minutes, I am able to leave the stall. I splash some water on my face and look in the mirror. I hardly recognize myself. I have let myself go. I have to get a handle on my life but I have no idea how to do so. I have been hoping a sign will come to let me know what to do next. But what if that is just an excuse to give myself a pass on my shitty behavior? What if this is the sign – almost having a panic attack in a supermarket over happy children?

I leave the restroom, ready to get my grocery shopping done without further incident. By the time I leave the supermarket, I am feeling grounded again. Sometimes my head gets the best of me. I decide I'll brush it from my mind and go get a coffee. I haven't bought anything frozen, so I don't need to get home right away. My inner chef refuses to die, so the thought of making a frozen meal still does not appeal to me, even with how depressed I am.

It has been a while since I have treated myself to an overpriced iced coffee. But today is quickly becoming a day that is unlike the others so I head into the coffee shop, trying to ignore the small crowd standing in line to wait. I find myself lost in thought at the menu, which seems to have doubled in items since the last time I was here.

Someone taps on my shoulder, and I nearly jump out of my skin. I take a deep breath and turn around, fearing who it will be.

If you enjoyed this sample then look for **Star Bright, Book 1 by Carla Coxwell**.

Other Books by Darla Dunbar

- The Romeo Alpha BBW Paranormal Shifter Romance Series

- Romeo Alpha Blood Lines Romance Series

- The Alpha Feud BBW Paranormal Shifter Romance Series

- The Daemon Paranormal Romance Chronicles

- The Mind Talker Paranormal Romance Series

- The Leather Satchel Paranormal Romance Series

Get the latest update on new releases from the author at:

https://darladunbar.com/newsletter/

About the Author - Darla Dunbar

Darla has been interested in paranormal romance since she was a teenager in high school. It was then that she discovered she could fulfill her fantasies through her writing.

Observing people and human behavior in the area of romance has always been one of her favorite pastimes. Combining that with an overactive imagination is a sure fire way of coming up with interesting themes.

Connect with Darla Dunbar

I really appreciate you reading my book! Here are my social media coordinates:

Friend me on Facebook: https://www.facebook.com/darladunbar/

Follow me on Twitter: https://twitter.com/DarlDunbar

Check me out on Goodreads: https://www.goodreads.com/author/show/8425857.Darla_Dunbar

Subscribe to my newsletter: https://darladunbar.com/newsletter/

Visit my website: https://darladunbar.com/